Fish catches man

and other short stories

by
Gene Luptak

Luptak Enterprises LLC

dba Ponderosa Pine Press   Pinetop, Arizona

This edition was prepared for printing by
Ghost River Images
5350 East Fourth Street
Tucson, Arizona 85711
www.ghostriverimages.com

Cover design by Studio 602, llc.
info@studio602design.com

Back Cover photo by Dawn Luptak.

ISBN 978-0-9759005-1-2

Library of Congress Control Number: 2008932117

Printed in the United States of America

July, 2008

10 9 8 7 6 5 4 3 2 1

Contents

Part Two – People

Part Three – Places

Part Four – About This Book

Part One – Snippets of Life

Little Buddy

The bus from the outside world came into Albufeira daily at 6:30 p.m. and Little Buddy didn't notice the young man with a backpack stepping off the bus.

Little Buddy is a brown and black dog; motherless, fatherless and homeless. As far back as he could remember he always had to scrounge for a living. But, he was small and didn't eat much. Unlike the lazy dogs that hung around the fish market in this tiny Portuguese town, Little Buddy preferred the beach. He was the first one – human or animal – there in the morning and the last one to leave in late afternoon.

The next morning after the young man arrived in town, Little Buddy didn't notice the man sunning himself near the large rock at one end of the boomerang-shaped beach. Little Buddy romped and played with the other beach-goers. Some days, one of the beach bums would give Little Buddy some lunch.

The young man, a visitor to this land from the United States, was not much different than Little Buddy. He was parentless and had no home. He was not tied down to anything. A couple months before, the young man saw his life crumble before him. He withdrew his life savings to tour

Europe in an effort to salvage his wrecked life; to pick up the pieces, so to speak, and start anew.

His parents died when he was young, and he passed from relative to relative until he finally ran away. He worked during the day and went to night school. He had a good job as an assistant to the pay officer at a company in downtown Chicago.

He fell deeply in love with a secretary in Chicago, and they planned to marry in the Fall. But three months before the wedding, she jilted him, saying she didn't love him any more. She began dating a junior executive who lived in a high-rise apartment overlooking Lake Michigan.

The young man drank heavily, showing up to work late and even coming back to his desk intoxicated after a two-hour lunch. His boss fired him.

The young man decided to hate Chicago. He knew he could always get a job doing something, but first he just had to go away somewhere and get himself together. He knew it would take time to forget the girl he once loved. He also realized that the answer wasn't in the bottle, a hard-hitting fact that came to him after he got fired. He took his life savings -- the money he saved so faithfully from every paycheck for months. He had planned to use the money for his marriage, and a down payment for their first home. Instead, he bought a one-way airline ticket to Europe, pocketing the rest.

He hoped when he came back to the United States he would have gotten his life together in one piece. He would start anew somewhere, anywhere except Chicago. He couldn't face that city again.

The young man first settled in London for a couple weeks, and then visited Paris. When he arrived in the Portuguese village he still felt depressed. Life still had no meaning for him. *Was living worth it?* He thought.

On the third day in Albufeira, the weather turned cold and there were no beach-goers that day. Little Buddy sat on the beach by himself. The young man walked to the beach and sat down near the large rock and stared out to sea.

Little Buddy ran to him and playfully barked and hoped the young man would play with him. But, the man didn't; he just stared out to the sea. Little Buddy curled near him and the two of them spent the afternoon together. The young man hardly knew he had a companion that day. He ignored Little Buddy.

The next day, the weather turned warmer and the beach-goers were again down at the beach and Little Buddy played with them. Toward late afternoon, the dog saw the young man sitting near the rock and went to him. The young man gently stroked Little Buddy's ear and scratched his chest, but he still looked out to the sea.

As the days went by, Little Buddy spent more time with the man near the rock. Once in a while, the man would play with him, throwing a stick into the water and Little Buddy would run after it barking happily. Each day, the man would come to the beach with a bottle of wine, several small, hard-crusted rolls and a package of cheese. He sometimes shared a small morsel of a roll and cheese with Little Buddy.

On the 10th day, the man walked down to the beach and Little Buddy ran happily up to him and the man gently rubbed his ear and ran down the beach letting the little dog run and bark at his heels. But the man didn't stop when he came to the rock but kept going to the far end of the boomerang-shaped beach. Little Buddy followed.

Soon, they walked off the beach and into the rugged cliff terrain. The man walked the dusty path and Little Buddy followed. They walked for more than an hour and once while the man was climbing down a steep ledge that was much too steep for Little Buddy, the man picked the dog up and carried him.

The dusty trail turned into a gravel road that led to another fishing village. The man stopped at a café and bought a bottle of cold mineral water. He poured some of the water in his cupped hand and let Little Buddy lap it up.

But the dogs in this village weren't friendly to Little Buddy. They didn't like Albufeira dogs so Little Buddy hid under a chair a few yards from where the young man sat inside the café. The other dogs kept their distance and finally went away. Little Buddy rested his head on his front paws. The long walk tired him, and soon he fell asleep.

When the young man finished the bottle of water he went outside to look for Little Buddy. He didn't know the dog had curled up under a nearby chair inside. He thought the dog was playing with the other dogs.

The young man walked to the beach out of sight from the café.

Little Buddy awoke. He looked for the young man but he wasn't in the café. He went outside. A big, black dog growled at him and suddenly a red dog attacked him. Little Buddy yelped and broke loose and ran from the dogs up the dusty road.

Several minutes later, the young man walked back to the café and asked several townspeople if they had seen a little brown and black dog that followed him to this village. They hadn't, but they helped him search the village for the dog. After an hour, the young man gave up.

"Why are you so concerned about a little mutt?" one tourist in town asked him. "No one will miss him; he's only a stray dog and they're hundreds of them in this area."

The young man returned to his Albufeira rented-room. The next day, he walked to the beach early and spent the entire day sitting near the rock. Little Buddy wasn't there.

The second day the young man returned to the beach hoping Little Buddy would be there, but he wasn't. About mid-afternoon, the man heard a yelp, and when he looked up he saw Little Buddy running towards him. The man jumped to his feet and ran to the dog, hugging him for a few seconds and playfully stroking his ears. The young man and Little Buddy played on the beach the rest of the afternoon; Little Buddy barking and splashing in the water chasing whatever the man would throw. The man smile and laughed as the two of them played together.

The young man and Little Buddy spent a few more days

on the beach playing together. But one afternoon, after their playing time had ended, the young man picked Little Buddy up in his arms and hugged him tightly and then put him down. The man walked away.

The next morning, while Little Buddy ran through town to the beach, the bus taking people to the train station passed him. The dog didn't notice it.

Little Buddy stayed near the rock all that day but the man didn't show up.

The young man and Little Buddy never saw each other again.

Ford and Me

My vacation this summer wasn't exotic. I had some real estate business to attend to in Grand Rapids, Michigan. I lived alone in a motel with kitchenette for $44 a night, and I had way too much time on my hands.

While thumbing through a Grand Rapids travel magazine, I learned that the Gerald R. Ford Presidential Museum was only a few miles down the road. Bored, I paid a visit to the memorial of our 38th president.

The place was huge, and I learned way more than I wanted to know about Ford. Do you know he never was elected president? He also served as vice president, and he wasn't elected to that office either. He just kind of slid into those roles.

He has Richard Nixon to thank for his high stature. When Nixon's vice president Spiro Agnew had to step down for accepting bribes when he was governor of Maryland, Nixon appointed Congressman Ford as his vice president. And, when Nixon resigned because of his Watergate cover-up, Ford became our national leader and commander-in-chief. When he ran for president as an incumbent, he lost to Jimmy Carter. About the only thing Ford ever did of note while president was to give his former boss, Richard Nixon, a full pardon.

Even so, Ford has a museum in his honor.

Why, in fact, does any president deserve a museum? Maybe the great ones do such as Washington, Lincoln, Roosevelt (both Franklin and Teddy) and Reagan, but not the minor ones like Clinton who was impeached and Ford who was never elected to the highest office in the land.

That got me thinking. I pay my taxes and I do my civic duty by showing up to vote and serve on juries. How about a museum for a lowly, hard-working, taxpaying-civic minded John Q. Public? If Ford deserves a museum, then I deserve one, too – "The Eugene Martin Luptak Loyal American Museum."

That's when I put these words and thoughts and convictions into action. On my property in Pinetop, Arizona, I have a tool shed -- a 12-by-18-foot building that is separate from my house. I decided to convert the tool shed into a museum to honor me personally, but also a symbol to honor the common American loyal citizen. I will pay my own way to build this – no tax money. I'm sure some tax money help fund Presidential museums.

I paid a contractor friend to help me convert the tool shed. We insulated it, raised the rafters so I could put in a ceiling fan, dry-walled it, painted it and carpeted it. Another friend made a red-white-and-blue "Eugene Martin Luptak Loyal American Museum" sign and we hung it over the door. Then we saluted the sign.

What to put in it? In Ford's museum, he exhibited the actual Watergate burglary tools. I'm not sure why Ford did this; the tools should be in Nixon's museum. So, I went searching. I decided to exhibit what the average Joe can do to prevent a burglary. On a shelf I displayed a deadbolt lock, window locks, a picture of a vicious-looking German Shepherd, light bulbs, and alarm-system sign and, if all these should fail, a double-barreled shotgun.

Ford displayed his (1) important papers, (2) gifts from foreign heads of state, (3) a 1970s gallery with video sound bites, bell-bottom jeans, love beads and eight-track tapes, (4) displays of his early childhood and his first job in his father's paint and varnish company, (5) a re-creation of the Oval Office and fancy holographic look at 10 different rooms in the White House, (6) State Dinner table and (7) White House Switchboard.

For important papers, I accumulated and displayed on my museum wall my birth certificate, wedding license, my third-grade "good reading" diploma, copy of my letter to the IRS explaining why my check to them bounced, and a note from the bank that my pickup with rear gun-rack had been paid in full.

I had a problem with gifts. I don't know any foreign heads of state. My neighbor who was mayor of Pinetop years ago gave me a plastic paper weight with a scorpion embedded in it, and last year I walked away with a black-velvet painting of Elvis at a Christmas gift-exchange party.

I didn't want to duplicate Ford's 70s decade, so I decided to focus on the 60s. I displayed my Army dog-tags (I served active duty for two years in the 60s and that's another reason I deserve a loyal American museum); a Beatles album cover; a Nehru jacket I dug out from the back of my closet; a picture of Martin Luther King Jr. giving his Famous "I Have a Dream" speech; pictures of my one-year trip bumming around Europe in 1968; "Ban the Bra," "Don't Trust Anyone Over 30" and "Turn On, Tune In, Drop Out" buttons; a Haight-Ashbury street sign; a vial of purported mud from Woodstock, and photo-copied, autographed pictures of astronauts Neil A. Armstrong and Edwin E. Aldrin Jr. (the first men who walked on the moon).

Memorabilia of my childhood and first job include a vial of my baby teeth that the Tooth Fairy didn't take; my baby book that recorded my first word as "mawferms"; my high school letterman's jacket; a picture of my first car (1950 Ford with shrunken head dangling from the rearview mirror); my 1956 high school yearbook turned to the page the prom queen wrote a note to me and calling me "George" instead of "Gene", and a $1 bill (that represented my first job selling tulips I picked from my mother's flower garden to neighbors.)

I can't afford holographic stuff, so I can't compete with Ford showing all those White House rooms. Who needs a holograph when anyone can see my one-room museum?

However, I can compete with Ford's State Dinner table complete with bone china, linen napkins and fresh flower centerpiece. On a card table I displayed butterfly placemats, fancy white paper plates and an arrangement of assorted colorful plastic flowers.

Ford's White House's switchboard has dozens of holes and switches with wires crisscrossing spaghetti-like. My "switchboard" is simple. I show off my Goofy animated phone I bought at Disneyland.

I think I will send the Ford Museum my goofy phone. The whole idea of him having a huge museum is goofy.

He Awoke

He awoke, though he kept his eyes closed. A strange sensation bolted through his body. He couldn't explain it, but as soon as his mind adjusted to the dark surroundings he felt a sense of insecurity and helplessness.

Through some physiological process, he could force air into his body. He winced at every breath because the air had a strong, almost gagging, odor. He was weak. Several times he felt like going into another seemingly endless sleep. He forced his eyelids to flutter a few times before opening them. Everything was pitch black. He glanced in different directions. Still, nothing but black. He couldn't see a thing, not even a faint image of anything.

Fear struck him. Walls pinned his body. He couldn't move. The walls engulfed him. No matter which part of his body he tried to move it touched a wall. The only good thing, to this point, was that he could move his head. He turned his head from side-to-side, only staring into darkness. He squirmed a bit, and the walls moved. He tilted, lying slightly on one side. Fatigued, he closed his eyes. Sleep descended upon him again.

He awoke. Through his fogged mind he faintly remembered something of his past. Not much, though. He desperately tried to piece together the cloudy thought of what went on before. He remembered being pinned against walls in his dark tomb. And, yes, the walls – they moved. But most of his past thoughts, and even those he focused on now, centered on whether he was alive or dead. He knew he lived before because a thought must be part of life. He convinced himself he couldn't be dead because death is the stoppage of all remembrances. Through his mixed-up mind he convinced himself that a line clearly could be drawn between life and death. Sometimes he was on one side of the line and sometimes, it seemed, on the other side. Was sleep part of death? At this moment, though, he was on life's side. It seemed that every time he was on this side he always had the same thoughts. Where was he? Who was he? Was there more to life, or death, than this? He again became aware of the walls pressing against his sides. He definitely was more than just a thought process. He definitely had a body, but he didn't know what it looked like. He wondered what kind of a life, or near-death, he was passing through. The thought struck him that maybe life, or death, isn't a passing thing. Maybe life and death stands still and now he is experiencing both of them in some type of a stationary form. Trying to reason things out only tortured his already confused mind. It was no use. He couldn't think clearly. All his thoughts whirled around in his mind. With his weakened condition, his head seemed to be spinning. The only thing real to him was the experience of some kind of existence.

Then, another thought came to him. This thought, actually, was an urge to do something. He just had to act on this instinct. He couldn't explain "instinct", but this inward desire was too great to neglect. Does having a feeling of instinct means he was a little farther on this side of life? Somehow, he had to get out of his enclosed prison. That was the urge that consumed him now. Instinct told him to hit the wall again and again. He didn't know why, but an uncontrollable force compelled him to fling his head against the wall in front of him. Since the rest of his body was pinned, it was the only thing he could move.

He forcefully hit the front of his head against the wall. Not all of his head touched it, though. Something was attached to his head – something that protruded out and only the end of it touched the wall. He hit, hit, hit. The wall moved. He did, too. His weight shifted to his left side. More pressure from the wall pressed against his left side. His right side of his body experienced less pressure. He kept hitting his head against the wall. Was he making progress? He didn't know. The urge to hit became more intense. He tired easily, and, again, fell asleep.

He awoke. The desire to escape his dark dungeon became stronger than it had been before. What's outside these walls? More darkness? More walls? More breathing room? Hit, hit, hit, and the wall spoke. He never heard that kind of a sound before. He previously only heard the "thud, thud, thud" when he hit the wall. This time after the last "thud" the wall spoke. Just a brief word – one syllable. He had no idea what the wall said. He hit it again, and, again, the wall spoke. Hit, hit, hit. He tired again, sleep overcame him. This process of sleeping, waking, hitting, and once in a while hearing the wall speak, continued for quite some time. The eighth or ninth time after he awoke, progress was made. The wall made a loud grunt, and suddenly something poured into his chamber. It was now bright, not pitch black that he was used to. Something was outside the wall. He could see an object through the hole in front of him. A slight breeze of a different smell came through the wall. It was more neutral. It didn't stink. He turned his head and stared away from the hole. Things were in his once dark chamber. He could see them, although he didn't know what they were. There were different colors surrounding him.

He knew he had a body but couldn't see much of it. He closed his eyes, darkness returned and he relaxed. Did he fall asleep again? He didn't know. The urge to hit the wall had controlled his mind. He hit, hit, hit, and the hole got bigger. The wall seemed to weaken and part of his sides now could move. He struggled, not only flinging his head to enlarge the hole but thrusting his sides against the weakened wall. The wall spoke again – this time a long, groaning sound. He felt freedom. His body moved and he pushed his head through the hole. He took a deep breath and stretched his sides as far as he could. His one side became free from the wall. He pushed and pushed, resting until strength returned and he pushed and flung his body again and again against the crumbling wall. Finally, the wall collapsed and he tumbled out. Light was everywhere. He stretched. He was totally free.

He looked around. Standing just a few inches away was a strange creature. It had fluffy, yellow fur and long skinny legs with claws for feet.

Just like him.

Fish Catches Man

Jim Brown, the owner of the local pet crematory, frowned at the large fish on his desk. He scratched the back of his head.

"You want what?" he asks.

"I want you to cremate this," says Henry Hitchcock, an assistant professor in the local university's marine department.

"But this is a huge fish," Brown questions.

"I know. This was a very special fish. I doubt there ever will be another one like him."

• • •

Maude sipped her coffee at the breakfast table and looked over the top of her morning newspaper and out the window. She saw the trail leading to the farm's pond had tall weeds blocking her view of the water.

"Hey, Homer, you better buy some herbicide and get rid of the weeds by the pond. Grandkids will be comin' in couple weeks and they need some shoreline to fish."

Homer, her husband, put down a piece of toast and lifted

a coffee cup to his lips. "Yeah, Okay," he grunted. "I'll do it tomorrow. I got to plow 20 acres for wheat today."

The next day, Homer drove into town to the farmers' co-operative and bought the strongest herbicide in stock. He drove 25 miles back to his farm and headed to the pond, pressing down a tangled web of chest-high weeds. He parked just a couple feet from the pond's shore.

I could plow the weeds with the tractor, but the weeds will just come up again, Homer thought. "*I'll kill 'em this time to the roots.*"

Homer lifted a five-gallon bucket of concentrated herbicide from the bed of the truck. He read the directions: "dilute 10 gallons of water for every quart of solution." He unscrewed the lid and took it off. He flinched, smelling the strong odor from the herbicide bucket.

"Oh, damn," Homer yelled. "Forgot to get a new sprayer at the co-op. Got to go into town again."

He kicked a pickup tire, swung the door open, crawled inside and cranked the engine. He flew backwards a foot to turn around, and sped off. He didn't notice that when he backed up, the truck knocked over the herbicide bucket and the contents flowed into the pond.

• • •

It was about the time the grandkids were planning to come to the farm that Homer called the university's marine department. Henry Hitchcock answered the phone.

Homer explained what had happened two weeks earlier and now dead fish were floating on top of the pond.

"The Prof is gone for a few days, but I'll drive out right after work and check it out," Henry promised.

As true to his word, Henry drove to Homer's farm that day. He surveyed the pond and the dead fish that had washed ashore. He scooped a sample of the water into a glass container. He gathered a few dead fish and put them in a bucket of water.

"I'll test the water to determine what's wrong with it, and I'll do an autopsy on the fish," he told Homer. "I'll get to the bottom of this yet. We may have to drain the pond, or maybe we can somehow filter the herbicide out.

"I'll come back tomorrow with some of my students and net the entire pond. Maybe there are still some live fish in it and we will move them someplace else."

The next day, Henry and three marine biology graduate students netted the entire pond. They caught five live fish, and dozens of dead trout, bass and catfish.

When Henry and his crew took the live trout to their marine laboratory in town, one of the students noticed that one brown trout was full of eggs. They emptied her and fertilized the eggs in a hatchery tray with the sperm of male fish. Weeks later, most of the eggs hatched. Hundreds of fry eventually grew into fingerlings.

Henry separated five of the largest fingerlings and let them grow to about 12 inches long. He began experimenting with them. Through ultrasound, one of the fish had a larger brain than the others. The lobes of the brain that controlled keen eyesight and smell were abnormally large.

Henry explained to his assistants that different fish have different parts of the brain more developed than others. A catfish has a keener sense of smell than it does eyesight. That's why people use smelly bait to catch catfish.

A trout, however, has a keener sense of eyesight than of smell.

Henry held up a model of a fish and told his students that fish has a lateral line down its side that contains sensory organs of smell. A fish smell from the length of its body and not from its "nose," he explained.

Henry showed the ultrasound pictures of his prized brown trout – the one with an enlarged brain – to the students.

"This, obviously is a mutated fish," he said. "The herbicide that spilled into the farmer's pond affected the fish, and especially the fish we took the eggs from. This offspring is a very special fish."

Henry and his students studied the mutated fish for two or three more months. They noticed that it did not swim in a school like the others, but was standoffish. It didn't gobble the hatchery food like the others did, but cautiously nibbled at it before taking a bite.

Henry surgically put a radio transmitter in the fish and also an electronic "pit tag." It is similar like putting a chip inside a dog or cat so it can be traced.

When the fish, which Henry named "Junior," was 20 inches long, he placed it and dozens of other trout into a transfer container and drove to Big Lake, which was the largest lake in the state. The lake is cold and deep enough for trout, and especially brown trout that were more aggressive and hardier than most other trout.

During the next three or four years, Henry and his graduate students monitored Junior. Fishermen never caught him. He rarely swam near the shore but stayed out in the open waters. If a boat was near, Junior swam away.

About once a year, Henry would locate Junior and "shock" the water and Junior and other fish would rise to the top. Junior was huge compared to the other fish. Junior was measured and then released. Henry didn't think Junior would ever be caught, and the fish would eventually be the state's record brown trout -- maybe the world's. And Henry was right, through the years Junior never got caught.

• • •

Junior always knew he was different. While other fish in the lake swam around aimlessly, gobbling up whatever was before them, Junior always cautiously scrutinized what he ate. He learned early that what looked and smelled tasty might be dangerous. His early recollection after being placed in the lake was watching one of his tiny brothers gobbling a mass of orange and green stuff and immediately being pulled up and disappearing forever out of the water.

He determined the world was not only water, but there was something beyond his liquid environment. What could it be? The other fish in the lake could care less. Sure, fish don't audibly communicate with each other, but to various degrees they are aware of what is happening with other fish and themselves.

Junior once looked up to the older fish in the lake that were bigger than he was. It didn't take long before he surmised that…well, the other fish in the lake were pretty stupid. They couldn't analyze a thing. As time went by, they, too, were pulled up out of the water and Junior never saw them again.

Junior was curious all the time. He knew he was placed in this watery world for a reason. "Who Am I?" he thought. "What Am I Doing Here?" "What Is The Purpose Of My Existence?" "Is There Something That Created Me?"

Junior didn't know he was mutant – a freak of nature. Being different than the other fish only made him lonely. One time, he thought he would end it all by eating that mass of orange and green stuff and be pulled away from his watery prison. He didn't belong in the lake, he thought, but belonged with other fish that were as intelligent as he was. If there are any.

However, his desire to live won out, and he never grabbed the orange and green smelly stuff. It obviously was artificial and came from the world above the water. He learned to eat only live things such as tiny bugs floating on top of his liquid world, various forms of plankton and the eggs other fish lay. He carefully looked at the morsel of food before he nudged it with his lips. Then, he would take a tiny nibble. If anything seemed out of place, such as some foreign object mixed up in this morsel, he immediately turned and swam away.

One time, Junior saw a squirming brown worm floating off the lake's floor. Junior examined this new source of food (it really smelled good) but another fish brushed him aside and gobbled it up. That fish gurgled, and then frantically swam away real fast. Something was pulling him to the shallow part of the lake where the water ended. This fish fought and pulled but it was no use. Junior swam close enough to the fish and saw a stringy thing hooking into his friend's jaw that was pulling him. Junior watched this fish disappear out of the water. *What did this to him?* Junior wondered. Junior learned never to nibble at anything that had strings attached.

• • •

Several years after Junior was released in the lake, Henry and his oldest son, George, 17, drove to Big Lake for the annual "shocking" of the water and to examine Junior.

"Holy Cow!" George exclaimed when Junior rose to the top of the lake. "That's the biggest fish I've ever seen. Let's take him home, filet him and have a feast?"

Henry laughed. "Not on your life. This is a very special fish that's smart enough to survive in its very hostile water. I think I will let it die of old age. Maybe I'll take it back to the marine pond at the university and showcase it"

"Why?" George questioned. "It's just a fish. It looks like this fish got into your head and it caught you instead of you catching it. I think we should eat it. We can invite the entire neighborhood.

Henry chuckled again. He knew he was attached to this fish, a freak of nature second to none.

"You know son," Henry said, "there is a true story about a man couple of years ago who was spear-fishing in the ocean and he hooked a huge groupie, about 100 pounds. That fish swam to the bottom and the man's hand got tangled in the heavy line. The fish went into a crevice and stayed there. The man couldn't untangle himself and he drowned."

"I guess the fish caught the man," George responded.

Henry chuckled again. "Talk about fish catching man. There's this huge building in Wisconsin at a fish museum that's shaped like a muskie. I think it's four-stories high. People can walk into it and view some fish artifacts, and actually stand at a lookout and see the town inside the fish's mouth. Talk about people being inside the belly of a fish. A modern-day Jonah and the Whale story."

George was not impressed. "I think we should eat this fish," he said, as his dad grabbed a travel-container from the boat and scooped Junior into it. Junior headed back to his first home, the university marine laboratory.

• • •

Junior refused to eat artificial or hatchery food, so Henry had to make sure he had live worms, bugs and plankton to eat. A few other large fish were in the same pond and they ate anything in sight.

Henry spent hours observing Junior swimming in the crystal-clear water. Junior could see Henry's image above his tiny watery prison. He watched as Henry tossed food to him. He developed trusting this man.

As time passed, and after hundreds of people came to look at this huge fish, Junior just gave up on his lonely life and just wanted to end it all. He mastered his world, he thought, and there was nothing left to experience. He refused to eat.

Early one morning, when Henry arrived at the marine department, he immediately walked to Junior's special indoor pond. Junior had died overnight and was floating on top of the water.

A wave of emotion swept over Henry. He knew this day would come, but it was still hard to emotionally say "goodbye" to this special friend he cared for through the years. Tears welled up in Henry's eyes. He thumbed through a scrapbook of pictures and notes he kept on Junior. He looked on his office wall of a picture of Junior he had taken last year. Junior obviously was a world's record for a brown trout. Henry vowed never to seek that official record. Junior was much more than just a world's record. He also decided not to do an autopsy on Junior and measure his mutant brain lobes. *What's the use,* he thought, *the research is over. Only people here at the university will have access to this scrapbook.*

• • •

Ten years later, Henry had a massive heart attack at home and died. Several days later, after the funeral and his remains cremated, George and his two siblings (Henry had been divorced for 15 years) gathered in the lawyer's office for the reading of the will.

After all Henry's earthly possessions were given out, the lawyer read the last paragraph:

"I know this last request will sound odd, but I want it accomplished as soon as possible. By now, my cremated remains are in a box. I have placed Junior's cremated remains in another box which is in my safe deposit box at the bank. The key and address of the bank is in my top desk drawer at home. Mix Junior's ashes with mine. Go to Big Lake and sprinkle our remains over the lake, not along the shore but in the middle where Junior spent most of his life. This is best for the both of us. None of my biology peers anywhere in the world experienced what I did. My life and research on Junior exceeded my own professional expectations. Please don't fail me on this last request. I love the three of you. Goodbye. Dad."

I Loved you, Tammie

When I was 16, I worked at a church summer camp in northern Michigan nestled under pines and maples. The week-long "older" girls' camp had just begun. These girls were only a year or two younger than me. Bus-load after bus-load arrived, disgorging their lovely cargo. *WOW! I'm going to enjoy this week,* I thought at the time. Months later, I wished I never worked at this camp but stayed in the big city bagging groceries at my neighborhood supermarket.

I walked across the grounds approaching the office when a fellow-worker poked his head out of the door and yelled, "Hey, Mason, you goin' go swimming?"

I don't know what I said but I heard a girl say to me, "Why don't you?" I looked around and there were two girls. One was rather small and attractive. The other was taller and looked sorta "wild" with short, spiky hair. (This was in the 60s and wild women wore their hair like that then) I tried to act cool, but inside I was blushing. It wasn't every day, or even a week, a girl actually talked to me.

The next time I saw the taller girl was either that evening or the next one. The girls in her cabin were chosen to act as waitresses during the dinner meal. We four boy-workers had our own special table in the kitchen. During the middle of dinner, I had to go into the dinning room filled with 160 girls to get something out of a refrigerator. That's when I saw her the second time. When I past her on the way to the fridge, I decided to be friendly and speak to her: "Aah, they got ya workin' as a waitress?" She didn't say anything, but looked away. I felt like an idiot.

After dinner, I stood near the kitchen door and watched the girls file out. One girl walked up to me and asked if I liked Tammie. I didn't know a Tammie, but the girl said she was the one I had spoken to earlier near the fridge. *Oh, the wild-looking one,* I thought. I mumbled something and walked away.

Several times the next day, while I was cleaning the swimming pool, girls kept coming up to me asking if I liked Tammie. I tried to brush them off by giving noncommittal answers. Sometimes while I was working at the pool, Tammie would buy candy from the camp store and give it to me through the hole in the cyclone fence. I could tell she must have liked me but she never came out and said so. One evening, one of her girl friends asked me through the fence that Tammie wanted me to sit by her that evening at vespers. I turned down the request. It might not look right to the camp director and counselors.

One afternoon after my camp tasks were over, I walked to the swimming pool to watch the girls swim. I saw Tammie in her bathing suit. She had a shapely figure, unlike some of the other 14-year-olds at the pool. Tammie and her closest girlfriend showed up all the other girls diving. Tammie and her friend saw me sitting on the bench on the other side of the fence watching them. They began to giggle.

The week skipped by way too fast and soon it was Friday. The girls at camp pestered me by dropping hints that Tammie liked me. Late Friday afternoon while shooting baskets by myself, Tammie walked up to me. We began shooting baskets together.

We talked and got friendlier. She had just graduated from elementary school and I asked her where she was going to high school?

"Africa," she said. Her father was in the Air Force and stationed in Africa. In a couple of months, his family would join him.

We talked on-and-on and one topic led to another. Soon, she offered to wash my clothes. I agreed. I told her I would give my dirty clothes to her after chapel that night. We parted. I walked to my cabin. I don't think my feet ever touched the ground. I sat on the edge of my bed, a funny feeling inside. I never before felt this way. I kept asking myself? *"Am I in love?"*

That evening, shortly after dinner, I went again to clean the pool. I looked up and saw Tammie looking at me from the other side of the fence. She called me over to her. She sat down on a bench on her side of the fence and I sat down on a bench on my side. We faced each other. Then, without changing the expression on her face, she told me she loved me.

I couldn't say a word. My mind went blank. We sat there and neither of us said a word for what seemed like two long minutes. Finally, she broke the silence and said something. I don't remember what she said but I got my voice back. I blurted out that I thought quite a lot about her, too. I asked her if she would save me a seat next to her in chapel that night. I don't really know why I asked her that, but that was the only thing I could think of and I thought it was the appropriate thing to say. At that moment I really didn't care what the camp director and counselors would think.

I was really excited. At last, my first date.

That evening, I met Tammie outside the chapel. All the girls were there waiting to go in as a group. I was the only boy there and I knew every girl was staring at me. I didn't care.

After the service, Tammie and I went up to my cabin and I gave her some of my dirty clothes. I couldn't allow her to see my underwear. I walked back with her to about 50 yards of her cabin and said "good night." That was Friday. Lucky Friday the 13th.

The next day we met at the swimming pool as usual. She asked me if I wanted to go steady. I said I didn't know,

"You're goin' to be a long ways off in Africa."

"But It's only goin' be three years," she said.

And so from then on, we were goin' steady.

We had another date that night. I asked her again if I could sit by her in chapel. All that day I kept telling myself that I loved her and she loved me and…we should kiss.

I had a plan worked out. After chapel I would ask her if she would like to go to the old corral in the forest that was about 100 yards south of the swimming pool. And there, I would kiss her. I never have been kissed before, at least not on the lips.

Since we were goin' steady, I thought I should give her a gift to show her my love. I went to the bookstore and bought her a New Testament. It cost $4.75. It was a lot of money for me; I only made $3 a day working at camp. I thought, *What does money mean when you are in love?*

After chapel, I put my plan in action. I asked her if she would like to go to the old corral. She didn't know where it was. After we started, I discovered I couldn't find it in the dark. We walked through the forest. She was wearing a shoulder-less dress. It was chilly and she said she was cold.

I didn't do anything, like put my arm around her. But I did give her the New Testament and I told her I loved her and that she meant quite a bit to me. We walked again and a low-hanging limb hit her. We weren't too far away from her cabin and we heard some of her cabin-mates yell something to her. She wanted to go back to her cabin. She again said, "I'm cold." Again, I didn't hug her. We parted.

I slowly walked back to my cabin feeling awful. My feet heavily hit the ground and it was a chore to move them. *I'm a complete flop,* I thought. About an hour later while lying on my bunk feeling sick inside, one of the guys walked in and told me he saw Tammie at the camp store. She seemed to be in pretty good spirits. I started to wonder. *Maybe she didn't think I was a flop after all.*

Sunday, the day before girls' camp would break up, came. We were more or less together all day. The girls were playing in the all-star softball game, but Tammie instead washed and ironed my clothes.

A devotional service started at the outdoor campfire ring. I let Tammie wear my red-and-black high school jacket. Someone told me that was the appropriate thing to do when you go steady with a girl.

While at the fire service, some of the girls stood near the fire and gave their testimonies. Tammie said she became a Christian that week. I was proud of her. While I was going with her, I couldn't help but think that she didn't look "wild" anymore. *Her becoming a Christian was the reason for it,* I thought.

After the service, we walked toward her cabin. When we got to about 50 yards to it we said our "good-nights" and parted. I walked back to my cabin.

About half-an-hour later, I went out with one of the other workers who had to blow taps on his trumpet. When we came near the back of the chapel, we met Tammie and a couple of her girlfriends. Ken went on to blow taps but I stopped to talk to Tammie. Her friends walked away. She asked me if she could keep my jacket. I said, "Yes."

While we were standing there, we saw someone with a flashlight by the swimming pool. It must have been the camp director, we told each other.

I turned my head to look at the shinning flashlight and then it happened. It was so fast I didn't realize what happened until it was over. We kissed!

I still haven't figured it all out, but I think Tammie ran up to me and before I knew anything we were cheek-to-cheek. Then we kissed—on the lips. After that, which only lasted a second or so, we went back to cheek-to-cheek. I can't remember that during all that time if I ever put my arms around her. I can't remember if she held me either. I must have stood there frozen for the next few seconds after we kissed. Because when I came to, Tammie was almost to her cabin. I walked back to my cabin floating on air, again. Seeing my grin, the other guys in the cabin knew what happened. They kidded me how nice it was to be kissed. Even Ken chuckled: "he went out with me to blow taps but after he met his girl, I never saw him again," he told the others.

It was a wonderful evening. I didn't sleep much that night. All I wanted to do was stay up and daydream.

And then it was noon the next day. Tammie told me to sit and eat lunch in the dining hall and not in the kitchen. So, I did. I sat at the counselors table. We both could keep our eyes on each other while we ate. But I couldn't eat. This was the last meal for the older girls' camp. In about an hour, Tammie would leave to go home, about 250 miles away.

And then all too soon that hour was up. Our hearts were almost broken. We said our "goodbyes" and we promised each other we would write every day. I had a mixed-up feeling inside when I saw Tammie get on that bus. But while the bus driver was making last minute checks, I went to the side of the bus where Tammie was by an open window. She reached down and we held hands. Tammie said she was about to cry. All too soon the driver was ready to leave. We took our last look at each other. The bus pulled away. I kept watching the bus as it went down the road and around the curve. She was gone. That's all I could think of. *She Was Gone!*

The next couple of days went by very slowly. And then the letters started to come in. I received three letters from her the same day. She probably received that many from me.

One letter she said: "...I miss you very much. I cryed all the way home. Three years are going to be a long time for us to be apart. Remember when you 'kissed' me that was the happist time in my life."

In another letter, she wrote: "When I was in camp all of the boys told me you were the only sain boy their because you did not care for grils, but now you care for one gril and I still think you are sain."

In the same letter she said she was sending a ring so I would have proof of our going steady. In a couple of days I received the ring. It was a nice ring. But, I thought, it was odd to have "United States Army" engraved on it. Inside, it had some other guy's name etched on it.

In the swimming pool that I clean daily at camp were little bugs. I tried almost everything I could think of to keep them out. In Tammie's letters she kept mentioning the bugs. It was a private joke between us. We always chuckled when we mentioned it to each other when we were both at camp. Now, however, when she talked about the bugs in her letters, telling me not to catch any of them for any other girl, they didn't seem funny.

The letters kept arriving. The other guys in my cabin all had girlfriends. And all summer the girls would write to them. Each time one of my co-workers would get a letter he would cut a notch on the wooden headboard on his bed. The three other guys had a lot of notches. There wasn't a single notch on my headboard. But that would change. I started to notch. But the other guys were too far ahead, I never would catch up. Even if Tammie would have written three letters a day I might have a chance to win the contest of notches.

Another letter arrived. "Dear Don, I just came home from the pool, and their was so much clorine in the pool that my eyes were red, I guess I will have to come back and swim with the bugs. I sure miss you a lot. All the boys wanted me to swim with them, but I didn't because I care to much for you. I'm sure proud of our going steady...Do you think our love will last. I think if we belive in Christ it will last. Because I love you very much. We think about the same as each other I promis I wil not go around with any other boys, I have to go now so good by sweet hart..."

And then late in August, she sent two pictures of us that were taken by one of her girlfriends while at camp. I cherished them.

But letters weren't the only way of communication. One evening, the caretaker yelled at me to come to his cabin. I did. He told me I had a telephone call. Tammie was on the line. We said the same thing that we were saying to each other in our letters. I cherished hearing her voice again.

We kept writing letters every day. Once in a while she

would call me. Then one Sunday, another call came. This time she said, "Don, I have a big surprise for you. I'm going to see you tomorrow." I was flabbergasted. Each Monday a bus from her area comes to camp dropping off a bunch of new campers for the week and pick up those who had just spent a week. She was going to make the 500-mile round trip on a school bus just to see me.

The next day I was really excited. I waited impatiently. Finally the bus rolled in. I got to see Tammie, but only for about 10 minutes. We walked down to the swimming pool. We were both pretty quiet. Neither one of us felt like talking. Then all too soon it was time for her to go. I walked her back to the bus. Again, the bus rolled away with Tammie in it.

I turned my attention away from the bus and turned around. A male counselor about three years older than me stood there looking forlorn. He, too, had fallen for one of the girl campers that week. She and Tammie had just left on the same bus. I asked this guy what was wrong. He said, "You should know, you have a girl on there, too." I, though, had to say "goodbye" twice.

In one of Tammie's telephone calls she asked me if one of my co-workers who kind of fell for one of her girlfriends and I would drive to Grand Rapids and stay there for a couple of days. John and I wanted to go, but we didn't know how to do it. Neither one of us had a car.

My excitement mounted when Tammie wrote: "We (Tammie and her girlfriend) have a place for you and John to stay while you are hear and it wont cost a penny. Write and tell me if you are coming, and for how long...."

I guess I must have been confused. I didn't know quite how to act. I went to the telephone booth and called long distance to my mother. I told her I have a girlfriend and that John and I were going to Grand Rapids and stay there a couple of days. My mother sounded shocked. That weekend she and my dad came to see me. They didn't approve at all that I had a girlfriend. Especially that I was so serious about her. And, they didn't want me to go to Grand Rapids. After all, that was quite a distance from Detroit. I argued, but it didn't do any good.

My mother went through my clothes to see what needed washing. She asked me what happened to my red-and-black high school jacket. I hesitated, but then told her I gave it away. I can't remember what happened after that and I'm glad I don't remember. My mother was plenty angry.

• • •

Camp season was over, but I had to stay and paint buildings. I was awfully lonely. The other boys had gone home. I lived in the cabin by myself. There wasn't anyone except the caretaker and his wife within miles of that pine-and-oak-and-maple-infested camp. I cooked for myself. Once a day, though, the caretaker and his wife invited me to eat lunch with them. Most of the time he went to in a nearby Michigan town to see a doctor about his arthritis. They were pretty old, in their 60s, and even when they were around, I was still lonely. I cried once.

The evenings were really awful. I tried to occupy my time by carving a leather belt.

After a few days of this loneliness, I got all my change together and called Tammie. She called me five times and this was the first time I called her. That helped me not to feel so lonely after I talked to her. I felt better, for a while.

More letters came: "…Going steady is the next thing to bein ingaged to be married. I don't care do you?...God must want us to love because every thing has turned out the way we wanted it to. But if we brake up we know it is the will of God…I wanted to meat your mother and father but I was to late I guess…Ive been praying for us every night."

Sometimes I just couldn't believe this was happening to me. I never went with a girl before and didn't know how I should act and feel. Another letter: "Dearest Don, I sure miss you a lote, and now you miss me. How is it up their. If I know you your lonesome. I sure an lonely for you. I dream about you all most every night."

Another letter: "What would we do if their was not any mail serves or telephone...I have to talk to you and I can't say much in letters... You are the first boy and I hop you are the last boy for me, Don't you?"

Another letter came the next day. "Dearest Don: I just got up and found that my mother did not come home from a party she went to last night with a man named Jim. I don't know much about him and I don't think she does either..."

Then the letter of all letters came: "Dearest Don, the time has come for us to part for three years today. We got our 'port call.' I prayed and prayed that we could see each other before I left but I guess it is Gods will that this happened...I guess we did the write thing don't you about loving each other...We will be in Africa 13th, I will write to you but it is imposable for you to write to me untell I get to Africa. I will write to you every day but it takes two weeks for a letter to come all the way from Africa...."

And then came my last letter from her. "...I belive that we will serve him (God) lader on together...I guess I better go now but remember that I love you with all my Heart and I miss you very much With all my Love Tammie P.S. I love and miss you very much."

I was home at this time; my work at camp was over. Each day I walked to the mailbox and waited for the mailman. About two days after that last letter, I received a package from Tammie. Inside was a box of fudge. "Dearest Don I want you to sample my fudge Love Tammie" was scrawled on the back of a receipt.

That was the last I heard from Tammie. For weeks, I would wait for the mailman. No letters.

The weeks stretched into months.

The heart mends slowly.

She Was Eight and He Was Ten

She was 8, and attended a small mountain school. She was pretty with a turned-up nose and high cheekbones. At that time, she wore her blond hair in pigtails. The boys chased her around the school playground. She laughed and was happy. She and her two girlfriends played endlessly with dolls. She loved hikes with her father in the nearby woods.

He was 10, and attended a large grade school in a huge metropolitan area. He had dark, wavy hair and had a dark complexion. Girls tried to sit next to him in the lunchroom. He was happy-go-lucky, and he had a lot of friends who wanted to hang out with him. He and his friends made a spaceship out of cardboard boxes and they constantly imagined speeding out to space exploring new planets. He loved to go to movies with his mother.

She was 18, and had just graduated from the mountain's tiny high school. Only 11 graduates. She looked forward to getting a summer job at one of the town's two restaurants. Then in the Fall, she would travel 50 miles almost daily to attend junior college in a larger, mountain community. She wanted to become a registered nurse. Her older married sister lived in this larger town that now had six restaurants. She would stay at her sister's apartment once or twice a week so she wouldn't have the long drive back home after school.

He was 20, and worked as an ad salesman for the city's largest newspaper. He made good money, bought a fancy, bright-red car and partied much of the time. He and a roommate shared an apartment in a suburban town. He took a couple college courses but dropped out. He read philosophy books, and decided he would gain knowledge that way instead of going to college.

She was 23, and a nurse at the hospital in the town that now had eight restaurants. She still lived at home with her parents 50 miles away. She worked three, 12-hour shifts. She loved to cook and sew. She entered a dress in the county fair and won a blue ribbon. She had few dates; there weren't too many eligible bachelors around who qualified as husband-material. When she didn't work on Sundays, she helped out in the children's Sunday School at the small Baptist church in her tiny town.

He was 25, and he didn't live in the large metropolitan city any more. His parents moved to the mountain community that had eight restaurants. He lived with his parents. He wrote books, and already had one published. He had a job at the community's super-center store. People 75 miles around came to shop there. He was lonely; he had a couple failed flings in the large city. It soured him. He turned to his Baptist upbringing and studied the Bible. He hadn't had a date in two years; there weren't that many single women around in this mountain town. He was lonely. *Maybe he should move back to the metropolitan city,* he thought.

A mutual friend introduced them, thinking they were a perfect match. He thought she was very pretty with her turned-up nose and high cheekbones. She, on the other hand, was riveted with his dark, wavy hair and dark complexion. They hit it off right away and for more than two months they were with each other as much as five times a week. They made day-long drives back and forth to the metropolitan city to see the latest movie. She went with him when he bought books at Barnes and Noble and he tagged along when she shopped at Target. They had picnics in the woods near the stream, and she watched while he fished off-shore at a nearby lake. Once, they shared a banana split at the local Dairy Queen. They laughed and teased each other as they fed each other with the same spoon. They thought that was hilarious. He laughed so hard when he fed her that tears rolled from his eyes. They were very happy together and they hinted at marriage.

During the third month of their courtship, he began to have doubts about the relationship. It was too easy; she came on to him too strongly, he thought. Was he getting cold-feet? Could he find a different girl who read more and shared his deep philosophical thoughts? These questions tormented him for several weeks. He made the decision. One evening, he told her that it just wasn't working out and he knew they had no future together. She sobbed, and told him she couldn't stand him.

She was 35, and now lived in the mountain community that now had 12 restaurants. Her husband was a no-nonsense, solid type. He worked hard to support his wife and two children. He didn't do too many fun things. He was an elder in the Baptist church. She no longer worked as a nurse, but stayed home to raise her son and daughter. Once in a while, her mind would wander back and thought about the handsome man with dark, wavy hair. She wouldn't dwell on it though. Her son had soccer practice and she had to fix dinner.

He was 37, and now lived back in the metropolitan city. He had an apartment on the 27th floor with a beautiful view overlooking the nearby golf course. His sight was on the corporate ladder. He was moving up and always drove a new car. He had some serious relationships but they never lasted long. Some dumped him, and he dumped the others. Maybe one day he would find Miss Right.

He was 83, and he never found Miss Right. He was a committed bachelor, harvesting a commitment phobia. His health was failing; he had a stroke and was bound to a wheelchair. He could hardly move his arms and a nurse's aide had to feed him in the dinning room of Oakcrest Nursing home. His mind was still sharp, though. His nephew moved him there three months ago. Sometimes, the nephew visited him.

She was 81 and in poor health. Alzheimer's was consuming her mind. Some days she would recognize her loved ones; other days she wouldn't. Her husband had died 10 years before; she had four grandchildren with a great-grandchild on the way. Her daughter took her into her home, but it became too hard to look after her. She searched for a month for the best nursing home she could find. She settled on Oakcrest in the metropolitan city.

He was wheeled into the dining room at about 5 p.m. and pushed to a table. Across from him was a new patient he never had seen before. Her eyes were staring at her plate. She didn't even notice he was there. After a minute, though, she moved her head and he saw that she had a turned-up nose and high cheekbones. Her daughter was at her side and she reached for the spoon next to the plate. The man wanted to pick up the spoon instead and help feed her, but he couldn't. The daughter lifted the spoon to the old woman's mouth. That's when the old woman looked across the table for the first time and saw the handsome man with wavy hair.

Tears rolled from his eyes.

Her Idol

Lucinda moved excitedly in her theater seat, watching intently at the performers on stage. She was going to see her idol in person for the first time in her life. Only a few more minutes and he would appear on stage.

I looked at Lucinda and smiled. We had seats six rows from the stage. A glow came off Lucinda's face as she eagerly stared at the last act before Alfonso Flores would stride out.

Lucinda is a Spanish girl, an attractive 21-year-old who works as a secretary in Barcelona. She adores flamenco singing and dancing, and has boxes full of flamenco CDs and DVDs . Lucinda was vacationing in Seville when she heard her idol would perform in Almeria. She cut her holiday short, and boarded the 10-hour train trip to see him.

Afonso is a Spanish man, about 30 or younger, and, according to Lucinda, the best flamenco singer in the world.

Me, well, I'm American and I met Lucinda on the train, and she invited me to accompany her to the theater. I'm not important in this story. This was Lucinda's happiest hour.

The preliminary act concluded, and the announcer said something in Spanish and the crowd broke into cheers and loud applause. Lucinda shouted the loudest, it seemed.

Alfonso, a short man about 5-foot-7 and black wavy hair, sang for an hour. During a thundering applause, he pranced off stage. Lucinda's face was shining.

"Come on," she said. "I want to talk to him."

We walked backstage. I noticed there were no guards protecting the singer. Alfonso stood with a group of men near the dressing room door. Boldly, Lucinda walked up to him and started talking. She talked without even taking a breath. The other men walked away, and Lucinda and Alfonso stood and talked there for a long time. He then invited us to a private party after the second show that night.

Lucinda and I went around the corner for dinner and then came back for the second show. Alfonso had left a couple of tickets for us to get back in. Afterwards, we drove to the party, 15 miles away at some rich man's villa. I sat in the backseat of Alfonso's car as the singer and Lucinda were in the front seat. Lucinda sang flamenco songs that Alfonso had recorded. He smiled.

We only stayed about an hour at the party, which included about 50 of the singer's guests. Lucinda was an immediate hit; she sang and even danced as Alfonso played the guitar. We ate and drank, and Alfonso dropped us off at our hotel.

Before going to her room, Lucinda told me that Alfonso asked her to travel with him for the next four days while he was on a concert tour. She probably would have gone but I tried to explain to her what might happen.

"After all, he's a man and people will think you're his mistress," I explained to her. "But the decision is yours."

Lucinda looked puzzled for a moment, and then I could see consternation in her eyes. She nodded, and whispered that I was right. I knew after being with Lucinda for nearly two days on the train and in Almeria that she came from a very strict Spanish family and her morals were sky-high. I once tried to hold her hand and she smiled and wagged her finger at me. *She just got caught up with the excitement of the moment of being with her idol,* I thought.

We parted, and went to our separate rooms.

The next morning, Lucinda and I took her baggage to the train station since she was leaving at 1 p.m. Then we went to Alfonso's hotel because Lucinda wanted his autograph. She had forgotten to get it the night before.

She called him on the house phone, and Alfonso insisted she come up to his room...alone.

Lucinda hesitated to go to the room, but she really wanted the autograph very badly.

After discussing this with me for five minutes (I wasn't much help, I didn't know what to advise her) she decided to go to the room, but she would only stand in the doorway and get the autograph.

But it didn't work out that way.

I waited for Lucinda for 20 minutes, and finally she walked out of the elevator and into the lobby. I hurried to her.

"He has bad intentions," she told me in her broken English. She was a very dejected girl. I wanted to hug her, but I couldn't.

We walked outside and she told me when she knocked on the door Alfonso yelled for her to come in. She opened the door and the singer was sitting up in bed bare from the waist up.

"Pull up a chair and sit next to the bed," he told her. Lucinda refused, but lingered in the doorway. She said she didn't know what to do. Her years of idol worship had taken a plunge.

They talked for a minute, and another girl, a background singer in the show, walked in the room brushing Lucinda aside. She sat on Alfonso's bed. They held hands. Alfonso signed a picture giving it to the girl to hand it to Lucinda. Then, Alfonso shooed Lucinda from the room.

Lucinda didn't say much when I walked her to the train station. I felt sorry for her, and she had a hard time smiling at me when we said goodbye.

Before climbing on the train, she handed me the auto-graphed photo.

From Mexico with Love

The receptionist ushered Louis Martin, an ABC Television reporter, into Hector Perez's palatial New York City office.

"Mr. Perez will join you shortly," said the long-haired and shapely receptionist as she closed the door leaving the reporter alone in the office.

Martin glanced around the room, especially at all the diplomas and pictures on the wall – a B.A. from Ohio State University, a masters from Princeton, a slew of commendations from the New York Stock Exchange, NASDAQ and various investor clubs. Perez, a multi-millionaire on the threshold of becoming a billionaire (in the footsteps of Warren Buffett), illegally came to the United States from Mexico as a teenager. He worked in lettuce fields outside Yuma, Arizona, self-educated himself by earning a GED; attended college by working at brokerage firms, and, after graduation, made a mint as a short-term trader.

ABC wanted to profile Perez as a poor Mexican climbing atop Wall Street.

Martin stepped in front of a picture of three young boys and a dog and studied it carefully.

The door opened.

"That's me with the sling shot," Perez announced to his visitor, who turned and looked at Perez in his Italian suit, Rolex wristwatch and slick, black hair combed straight back.

"We all crossed the border illegally at different times," Perez continued. "Julio died of thirst in the middle of August in the Organ Pipe National Monument, and Pedro is doing especially well as a real estate broker in Los Angeles.

The reporter opened his notebook.

"I just want to ask a few questions before the TV crew arrives in about a half-hour," Martin said. "There are all kinds of news about giving amnesty to undocumented immigrants and I want to tell our audience the success story of a poor boy in Sonora who snuck across the border illegally and became a United States citizen through proper channels while at the same time beating the stock market. What motivated you to go from the lettuce fields to the boardroom, a trader and CEO of your own diversified company?"

"Sit down, and I'll tell you my story and the secret of my success," Perez said. "Some of it was just plain luck at being at the right place at the right time and knowing the right people who took me under their wings. But, I spent countless hours studying the market and charts and reading about others who had success in the market."

Perez settled down behind a huge mahogany desk, and Martin scooted a chair close enough to the desk putting his tablet on it to take notes.

"When I was 14 stooping and picking lettuce under 110 degrees, I naturally realized there had to be a better way to make a living," Perez began. "I wanted to live comfortably and also send money home to my parents and brothers and sisters.

"I remembered when the coyote drove us through downtown Phoenix I looked out the van window and saw those tall buildings and men wearing suits and ties with briefcases. I knew there was a better way to make more money than working the fields.

"After work I spent most of my time in the Yuma Library studying. There were some free classes and I learned better English. I asked the teachers all kinds of questions.

"After couple years, I realized to become successful I had to have only two things: a good education and work in a field that's closest to where the money's at.

"I thought about banking, but that was limited to whatever that particular bank had. Real estate was promising, but I came to the conclusion that there is more money to be made in the stock market than any place else. I set my goals to be a stock trader."

"That's good," Martin interrupted, "I'll ask you questions along those lines when my camera crew comes. We can go more in detail about how you educated yourself and how you worked through college. Maybe some of your early experiences working in a brokerage house."

"The time I worked for a broker was quite rewarding, but I also learned that I was making much more money for someone else than for myself," Perez said. "I realized I had to be my own boss and control 100 percent of the money I made.

"Actually, I learned that buying and selling stocks could be rewarding, but the bulk of the money I made through the past 15 years was option trading."

"I heard of options, but I really don't know much about them," Martin said.

"Most people don't; even some hardcore stock traders who have been in the business for decades really don't know the ins and outs of it. You can make much more money using options than buying and selling stocks. It is risky, but you can eliminate much of the risk by doing your homework -- studying the market trends, Where support and resistance are, examining company records and watching where the institutions are placing their money...the list goes on and on."

"Stock traders do that, don't they," Martin asked.

"Yes, but do they use Japanese candlesticks such as a Morning Star in a downtrend that does not need any confirmation but an inverted hammer does, or know what strike price to use, or decide if they should be either 'in-,' 'at- 'or 'out-of- the- money?' Do they know anything about using deltas to determine the relationship between the movements of the option compared to the actual moving of the stock? An option is a contract, but not the obligation, to buy and sell stocks. And options have expiration dates, stocks don't. Do they know what a Bull Put Spread is? How about an Iron Condor? Are they successful with naked puts? I watch very closely the Stochastics, moving averages especially the moving average convergence divergence. My favorite is a breakout of a Bull Flag. How about the RSI trading method? Or triple bottoms, Fibonacci Retracements, price channels, MACDs, Bollinger Bands and, most importantly that your broker won't tell you, where to place a stop loss to get in and to get out when the stock hits your target..."

"Wait a minute," Martin interrupted, "I don't have the faintest idea what you're talking about and neither will my audience. Maybe we should stick with your rise in the stock market but not the specifics on how to play it."

The office door opened and the long-haired receptionist poked her head in. "The TV crew is outside," she said.

"Let them in," said Perez, turning to Martin, "Let them set up while I go in my inner office and make an important telephone call."

Perez got up and left through another door near the picture of him with the sling shot.

He entered the small office, closed the soundproof door and reached for a phone on the table near a smaller mahogany desk. A few seconds later, his childhood friend, Pedro, was on the line.

"You never guess who's in my office right now," Perez

chuckled. "The ABC television crew wants to do a story on me from being an illegal to a successful United States citizen."

Both men laughed.

"If they really knew the truth they would have even a better story," Perez said. "The Americans think that Mexico is so corrupt that you have to bribe every official in Mexico to get anything done."

Perez laughed. "If they only knew it is the same here in the United States. How do you think we got our citizen papers – by bribing people in the Immigration and Naturalization Bureau.

"Yeah," Pedro chuckled. "United States, the land of opportunity. You can bypass the long, tedious legalization process and go to the front of the line if you have enough money to slip someone under the table. From Mexico with love, my friend...from Mexico with love! Viva Mexico! It is easy to beat the United States' monetary system. Most of the people born in the United States haven't figured it out themselves."

"I know," Perez said. "When I explained how to beat the market using options and advanced technicals, the reporter didn't have the foggiest idea what I was talking about.

"Americans say how stupid and lazy Mexicans are, but the Americans are stupider and lazier. They are so lazy they give their brokers and money managers their hard-earned money and ask them to make the money grow. And most of the brokers and managers pocket big chunks of their clients' money or charge them up to $200 for just one trade. I go online and only pay less than $10 a trade. Who's dumber? When I was a teenager I learned that to make real money I had to control it all by myself and not let others do it for me. If a dumb and lazy Mexican can figure it out, why can't most Americans understand that?"

Phoenix Smells

Phoenix needs a new identity. Sure, it has nice weather in the winter, but the hot, awful summer negates that. So, Phoenix is Zero.

After all, Boston has its baked beans, Fort Lauderdale its wild Easter parties on the beach, Milwaukee its beer, New York its big apples, Chicago its wind, Seattle its gourmet coffee, Oshkosh its overalls and San Francisco...well, you get the picture.

Phoenix needs something that is here 24-7 all year around that residents can be proud of and people from around the world can flock here to admire.

This something is right under the city fathers' noses.

I suggest Phoenix spend millions of dollars on "smell-stacks."

What? You ask. I'll explain later. Have you ever driven past a bakery and the smell of freshly-baked bread lulled you in such feel-good contentment that you forgot about the jerk who just cut you off?

Another example: When I lived in Milwaukee, sometimes there were several days in a row that the temperature never got above zero degrees. While walking several blocks each morning from the parking garage to work, I would pass a candy factory. Its smokestack spewed a rich chocolate fragrance. That walk was like inhaling a cup of hot cocoa. It made me forget how cold it was.

Phoenix should have dozens of smellstacks emitting smells throughout the city. A smellstack is similar to a smokestack minus the smoke. The Environmental Protection Agency, I'm sure, would approve.

Just think about it. Driving across town amid the heavy traffic and terrific heat wouldn't be much of a chore. Every few blocks the nosebuds would awake because of arousing aromas. For instance, near floral shops we would get a whiff of flowers; new car dealers the smell of the interior of a new car; near the many coffee stores the aroma of coffee; near lumber yards the scent of pine and cedar; near candy stores the bouquet of chocolate; near shoe stores the redolence of leather, and department stores the odor of perfume.

Even now, sometimes when you drive past a restaurant you get a faint smell of greasy food. A smellstack will enhance the smell 100 times. But instead of the hint of greasy foods, how about taking a deep breath of fried chicken, mesquite-smoked T-bone steaks, pizza and cinnamon rolls?

Smellstacks should especially be placed near the city's sewer treatment plant, dairies, landfills and septic tank cleaning companies.

Scientists for years successfully have been duplicating all kinds of smells. I used to work for a company that made food enhancements, and there was a cabinet in R and D with tiny bottles filled with colorful liquids. The bottles contained various scents of food. Once, a friend opened the cabinet door for me and in a matter of a few seconds I whiffed my way through a six-course dinner from appetizer to dessert.

Gallons of these potent liquids could be poured into a smellstack. A huge electric fan at the bottom will send the scent up the stack far and wide for all of us to smell.

With these smellstacks all around us, the city would finally have an identity.

Phoenix would be known as the Nostril Capital of the World.

The Rabbit

Little Tom Dudley couldn't sleep. It was 2 a.m. and he was still awake. His Dad will wake him up in four hours. They'll eat a man-sized breakfast and Little Tom will kiss his mother goodbye and Dad and Son will leave for the State Fair. Tom hardly could wait to enter his pet rabbit into competition with dozens of other rabbits from throughout the state.

Tom, 12, lived in Franklin, a farming village about 150 miles from Phoenix. He liked to visit the big cities of Phoenix and Tucson, making the trip to either place about once or twice a year. He enjoyed the city atmosphere, but always was anxious to get back to the farm.

Tom finally fell asleep, but when his Dad woke him at 6 a.m., it seemed he only had snoozed for five minutes, although he knew he had slept about three hours.

An hour later, Dad and Tom were in the pickup, with Sam, his pet rabbit in a small cage between them on the seat. Dad wanted Sam to ride in the pickup bed, but Tom insisted the highway wind might cause Sam to get a cold. Dad smiled and relented.

Tom waved goodbye to his Mom. He couldn't help but notice how pretty she looked today. She was wearing the green-stripped apron he had bought with his allowances and had given it to her last Christmas.

Just before they reached the interstate, Tom stuck his hand in the cage and whispered to Sam, "We're going to win a prize. You are a beautiful rabbit, and a tremendous pet." Dad sat silent at the wheel.

They arrived in Phoenix and went directly to Aunt Sarah's house. Dad would turn back to Franklin, but Tom would stay for several days while his rabbit was on display at the Arizona State Fair.

Before Dad left, he took the lad aside and told him not to get his hopes up too high on winning a prize at the fair.

"There'll be a hundred or more people entering rabbits in the fair, Tom. You entered Sam in the general competition and not in the youth category where you would have had a better chance of winning. Not everyone can win."

"I know I'm going to win, Dad, I just know it," Tom said. "I think Sam can compete with the best of them and that's why I'm entering him against rabbits raised by adults."

Dad hugged his son. "Here's $50 Tom, have a good time at the fair, and I'll pick you up in a week."

Tom stuffed the money in his overalls and watched his father turn the corner and drive out of sight.

Late that afternoon, Aunt Sarah drove Tom and Sam to the fair, where Tom signed papers and entered Sam into competition. The sign-in person led the boy to Sam's cage. Tom snuggled Sam for a minute before placing him in the cage. "I've been looking forward to going to the fair for a long time, Sam," he said. "But more important, I want to show the people the prettiest rabbit in the whole state."

Tom didn't sleep much that night, and the next morning Aunt Sarah drove Tom to the fair. He walked immediately to Sam's cage, the home for the rabbit the next few days. Tom imagined that in a few hours a blue ribbon would be hanging on Sam's cage. Judging would start in a couple hours. Aunt Sarah had an errand to run, so Tom wandered the fairgrounds. He couldn't remember if he had ever seen so many people at one time in all his life. He visited the booths, all of the farm animals, the midway, and watched a comedy show. He spent some of the money his father had given him for a hot dog and an orange drink.

The time for rabbit judging approached. Tom stood next to some big cardboard boxes, as close to the judges as he could.

The judges had several assistants to help them. The assistants got the rabbits from the cages and set them before the judges. The judges studied the rabbits, placing those they considered the best ones in special cages. They told their helpers to return the rest of the unlucky rabbits back to their original cages. About six rabbits were judged in each of the preliminaries at a time. It was lucky that even one of them made it to the special cage.

Tom waited patiently and then saw one of the assistants pick up Sam and place him before the judges. Tom held his breath.

A judge looked at Sam and grinned. Then he burst into laughter. "Hey, look here," he said to the other judges, "this rabbit is so shaggy that it would only be good in a stew pot. For the life of me, I can't understand why anyone would enter this specimen in a fair. Musta been a jokester."

The other judges joined in and chuckled. Most of the people in the room didn't hear the judges, but Tom did because he was so close to them.

At first, Tom stood motionless, his lips quivering. Tears then began streaming down his cheeks. He brushed them away with the back of his hand and ran toward the judges' table.

Tom snatched up Sam in his arms and hugged him close to his face. He glanced at the judges, turned and ran sobbing out the door.

The judges stood silently, each staring at the floor.

That night at Aunt Sarah's house, Tom called home and asked if Dad would come and pick him up tomorrow.

Runaway Boy

The tiny counter stool at Pete's Diner wheezed as Officer Ted Jenkins shifted his bulky 240-pound body. His butt overlapped the stool.

"Gimme another doughnut and more coffee, Pete. I'm really hungry this morning. The ol' lady wouldn't get up and fix me breakfast."

Pete walked to the far end of the counter. Jenkins sat alone in the diner. As Pete lifted the plastic lid over a pile of doughnuts, the door opened and a boy of about seven years old entered, carrying a hobo's stick over his right shoulder. A red railroader's handkerchief full of the lad's most valuable earthly possessions was tied into a bulging ball at one end of the stick.

Jenkins shifted his body again to look at the boy. The stool grudgingly again gave way and groaned. The policeman immediately thought he would have to take a police report and return the runaway to his parents. Or, maybe I'll just let the kid have his little adventure, Jenkins thought. I ran away from home a couple times myself when I was about his age.

The boy leaned the stick against the counter and climbed on a stool next to the officer.

"Gimme a strawberry milkshake," he ordered. "And put some whip cream on top."

Jenkins eyed the boy, who was wearing blue denims and a white T-shirt with the words "Grandma went to Disneyland and all she got me was this lousy shirt." Jenkins chuckled.

"Ya not running away from home, are ya?"

"Nope. Just taking off a couple days to go around the world. Might even stop in New York City."

The officer winked at Pete, who was smiling and leaning against the kitchen door. "Kids will be kids, I guess," Jenkins muttered to no one in particular. He took a bite out of his doughnut, and turned to the boy.

"Look kid, it takes money to go around the world, and New York is a thousand miles away. Lotsa money. Ya got any?"

"Yep. Just got myself a hundred dollars this morning. That's 'nough to go around the world."

Jenkins smiled and shrugged his shoulders. Kids! Pete set the milkshake down on the counter and the boy greedily began gulping it down. Jenkins took another bite from his doughnut, and the policeman and boy sat in silence.

The boy's straw sucked up the last bit of milkshake creating a gurgling sound. He hopped off the stool and picked up his hobo's stick.

"Well, I gotta go and start my trip. How much I owe you?"

"Seventy-five cents," Pete replied.

"Can you cash a twenty-dollar bill," the boy asked, reaching into his trouser pocket.

"Forget it, kid," said Jenkins wearily. "The shake's on me. Put the kid's bill on my tab, Pete. Now, run along and play."

After the boy closed the door behind him, Jenkins began chuckling. "I've always been a soft touch for kids. This one really got a wild imagination, doesn't he Pete? I remember once I ran away from home to go around the world. Got 'bout six blocks an' got hungry so I went back home. Bet that little jerk will be home begging cookies from his mommy before noon."

Jenkins turned his attention to the rest of his doughnut and coffee. Several minutes later, he sauntered from the diner and leisurely crawled behind the steering wheel of his squad car parked in front of the diner. He flipped the police radio switch on and picked up the microphone.

"Car 27 back in service."

"Ted, where've you been?" scolded the dispatcher. "I've been trying to reach you for 20 minutes. Get down to the Oak Street Variety Store and take a till-tapping report. Somebody walked out with a hundred dollars in twenties, and the manager says the only person he saw there at the time was..."

Long-nosed Workhorse

A couple decades or so ago, I went to the famed Ringling Bros. and Barnum & Bailey Circus in Chicago and settled down with peanuts in one hand, a bag of popcorn in the other, and a soft drink straddled between my knees. The band struck up and the circus began.

Oh, I watched the lion trainer, the trapeze artists, the dome of death motorcycle riders and all the others who got loud applause and major headlines. But, my eyes were actually trained on the huge elephant. He has carried more than his share of weight in the circus for years. I'm sure - - a real workhorse, so to speak. *What press does he ever get*, I thought.

It was only logical to talk to him to get the real scoop of what this year's circus is all about.

The next morning, I walked into the animal barn and approached the real star of the show. I introduced myself to George, shook his trunk and pulled my notebook out my rear pocket.

Me: I'm writing a book and I want to include an interview with you in it, George. First of all, why isn't the world-famous animal trainer Gunther Gebel-Williams performing?

George: He's with the red unit of the circus, and we are the blue. He's very good, but we've got some terrific animal acts ourselves. Out trainer, Axel Gautier, for instance, has taught us elephants to stand on our two back legs and walk backward. And our cat show is really different. Jerry Wegmann walks into a steel cage with lions, tigers, leopards, a puma and – get this – three St. Bernard dogs.

Me: You mean lions and tigers and dogs, all in the same cage?

George: Yep. This year animal acts are highlighted. I wish they would give us elephants more credit, though. Oh, well. I'm still glad the animals are getting their due. There are camels, zebras, bears, horses and a baboon show that's fantastic. One baboon actually jumps on a motorcycle and drives it around. I heard one bear ask the baboon to teach him how to drive a motorcycle.

Me: You mean a baboon and a bear can actually talk to each other?

George: What's so unusual about that? You're talking to an elephant, aren't you?

Me: Yes… You're really hyped about the circus, aren't you?

George: Why Not! I get tired of people thinking we aren't as good as the red unit. In some ways, we're even better. Do they have 16 Zulu warriors from South Africa doing war dances and blowing fire from their mouths? No!

Do they have Captain Christopher and Commander Weiss being shot out of double-barreled cannon? No!

Do they have the Tianjin Acrobatic Troupe from the People's Republic of China performing the grueling Chinese Web act in a mass of twisted leather straps near the ceiling?

And the Flying Vazquez Trapeze troupe. Miguel Vazquez performs the unparalleled quadruple somersault into the hands of his brother, Juan. And the men who sword fight and jump up and down on the high wire. And…

Me: OK, I'm convinced. You're better than the red unit. Now, what about the clowns?

George: I'm glad you asked. This is the 40th anniversary

of Ringling Bros.' Clown College, and the clown acts are big this year. They are reaching back into time and pulling out some of the best acts ever seen. Remember all the clowns piling out of the tiny car, and the firehouse stunt with hoses, ladders, hydrants and fire, and the crew of would-be painters slipping and sliding on spilled paint?

Me: There is something I always wondered about. Let me ask the most important question of all, George. Is it true elephants are afraid of mice?

George: Nonsense! I weigh nearly 7 tons and a mouse can't possibly scare me. But I'll let you in on a secret: the two pythons in the circus really scare me. At least they only appear for a few minutes, wrapped around two women during the fanfare. I keep my distance.

Me: George, I know you can go on for hours talking about the circus. But, isn't there anything that bugs you about it?

George: Well…I don't….Maybe! Yes! In the circus program there is this write-up for the aerial acts: "Absolutely Anxious Awesome Acrobatic Action Amazingly Achieved at Astonishing Altitudes Approaching the Apex of the Arena as an Appropriately Admiring Audience Applauds the Assemblage of Ambidextrous Athletic Abracadabra." All that alliteration! Isn't that great? We elephants want equal billing.

Me: Don't you believe that alliteration is too much hype?

George: Who Cares! That's part of the circus. You got to fill the seats or else all my animal friends and I won't eat. Would you do me a favor?

Me: Sure.

George: Would you print in your book a lot of alliteration for the elephants' act?

Me: I don't know. Well, I'll try. Let me think.... How about: "Paramount Prideful Pack of Pert, Ponderous Pachyderms Parade Painlessly Performing Pleasantly Past People Passionately Propelling Praises Profusely?"

George: What? Well, that's a start. Maybe there's hope for you as a writer yet. What's the name of your book?

Me: *Fish Catches Man.*

George: Great! Why not *Elephants the Real Heroes*?

Me: I'll think about it.

The Unicorn

Once upon a time, the Ringling Bros. & Barnum and Bailey Circus rolled into town and tried to pawn off on the public "a living unicorn."

"It's really not a unicorn," said spectators when they saw the "unicorn" being paraded around the center ring. "It's an old goat with a horn somehow glued to the middle of its forehead."

This made the goat, or unicorn, very sad. People laughed at him.

Don't they believe in me? He thought.

That night, when all the circus keepers were sleeping, the goat, or unicorn, mysteriously nudged the latch on his cage and the door opened. He crept out. He slowly walked past the other animals and crept out the main door, which had been left open a crack. Again, mysteriously.

The next morning, the keepers found the goat, or unicorn, missing; the door wide open. They hunted all over the grounds for about an hour but the animal wasn't in sight. When the keepers returned to the barn, they closed the door. That's when they saw a note taped on the door:

"My friend, the unicorn, has been very sad with your circus. Everywhere you go the people laugh at him. I decided

to take him home where he belongs – a planet far away. Once there were plenty of beautiful unicorns, some pastel green and yellow and blue and white on your Earth. But thousands of years ago some mean warriors from my planet came and stole all of them. I decided to bring a unicorn back to Earth, but the people there just wouldn't believe. I'm sad, too."

The keepers let out a wild cry when they saw who had written the note:

It was signed: "E.T."

Casa Jim's

A motley-looking group of about 20 bearded and shaggy-haired young people sat on chairs and on the floor at Casa Jim's "youth" hostel sipping beer. It was 1968, and the afternoon sun beat on the windows, causing the air inside the bar to be stale and forcing beads of sweat to form on the occupants' foreheads. It was siesta-time in this Spanish town of Compello, just north of Alicante on the Mediterranean Sea.

Hardly anyone stirred, and to talk was too much of an effort. Casa Jim's was not the typical youth hostel. It's mainly for college-age hitchhikers who stop at Compello, either coming from or going to someplace else. There's not much to do in Compello but to crash at Casa Jim's.

Jim Hawkins, a bachelor in his 30s and a disgruntled runaway from New York City's Greenwich Village, owned the place. Casa Jim's was known as the ideal place for hardened hippies and drop-outs from the United States and other European countries and Australia, South Africa and New Zealand to bond together and share ideas, tell tall tales and get advice on what towns in Europe, Africa and Asia to visit.

On this particular day, a scratchy record by The Beatles blared on the juke box. A skinny and stooped man, who looked to be in his mid-40s, appeared in the doorway. Jim, who was behind the bar, looked up.

"Well, I'll be a sonofabitch, if it ain't Kentucky," he boomed, stepping from around the bar and bear-hugging the man. "How the sheet are ye man?"

"Doin' okey, I recken," replied the man, slapping Jim on his butt. "Sheet, man, it's good tah see ya."

Everyone looked up, especially Jackson Horne, a University of Michigan sociologist major, who always made an attempt to drill people to see what make them tick. All of the hitchhikers went back sipping beer and into their own world of daydreaming, influenced by the scratchy voices of The Beatles' *Hey, Jude*.

Jackson kept looking at Kentucky and tried to size him up. Kentucky and Jim were engaged in a conversation augmented with four-lettered words. Jackson got up and sat down on the bar stool next to Kentucky. When there was a lull in the conversation, Jackson butted in:

"Excuse me, but how long have you been over here, Kentucky?"

Kentucky slowly turned to face his inquisitor. He stared at Jackson. Then spoke.

" Do I know you? Hell, eleven or 12 years, hell, I jest about forget."

For the next hour Jackson talked with Kentucky, slyly drilling him but still making the conversation interesting enough to make Kentucky talk from everything from his childhood to the broads he had in his younger days. The mere fact that Jackson plunked down 25 pasetas for cheap red wine helped Kentucky to loosen his tongue.

After the "interview," Jackson went to his bunk and wrote about Kentucky in his "character" notebook, leaving Kentucky at the bar to nurse his second bottle of wine.

Jackson was amazed that Kentucky was only 35 years old, although he looked 10 years older. Jackson's interest in Kentucky was to add more data about Americans who came to the Continent for a visit and stayed too long. You see them in the streets of Paris' Left Bank, the medina of Tangiers, a Greek isle and the non-touristy beach towns of Spain. They all passed the point of no return; they've all gone "native," so to speak. Most of them are alcoholics, getting enough money somehow to exist. They sell their blood at blood banks, and the hardy get skin grafts off their butts for much more money.

Kentucky served three years in the U.S. Army, serving at bases in the United States and Japan. At age 21, he entered college as an accountant major. Between his junior and senior years he came to Europe on a shoestring, hitchhiking tour. He's been here ever since.

After the summer of hitchhiking through 10 countries, he decided to stay in Europe just one more year working as a clothing store clerk in London. Then he would go back to the states for his last year of college. After all, he reasoned, a full year experience living in Europe is better than a year in college.

Kentucky only worked six months and then started traveling again, hitting the cheaper countries of Turkey, Greece, Spain, Portugal and North Africa. When he ran short of money he went to Paris and sold copies of the *International Herald-Tribune*.

The year went by quickly, and Kentucky decided to stay just one more year in Europe and then head back to college in the states. Much of his money went to drinking. He met a lot of young people like himself on the Left Bank and he enjoyed "whorin'" around with them.

Another year came...and then another...and another. Kentucky still lived in Europe, this time in Greece where it was cheaper than Paris. He worked only when he had to, that is only to buy food and liquor and someplace where he could sleep with a roof over his head. Many times he just slept on beaches or in parks on benches or under trees.

He worked his way to Spain, where he spent many days at Casa Jim's, and then drifted to Turkey. He took a steamer for Morocco where he lived in the medinas of Tangiers, Casablanca and Marrakech for three years. He moved back to Spain and stayed at Casa Jim's for six months. Jim gave him free board in exchange of working around the place. Then Kentucky drifted away to other parts of Spain and Portugal but he always came back to Casa Jim's to greet his friend.

Kentucky liked to talk, and most of the hitchhikers he met at Casa Jim's were enthralled listening to his many experiences traveling in Europe, Asia and North Africa. Most of the hitchers were young, just as Kentucky was when he first came over the Pond, and they were awed with the many "ways of life" they found throughout Europe. Kentucky relished the "awe" usually showered upon him by these young hitchers, at least when he was somewhat sober. But he usually got drunk and Jim had to put him on a bunk in the hall and let him sleep it off.

Kentucky now lived on a boat about 20 miles from Casa Jim's with another "comrade" and they fished for their food and scrounged for their booze and other necessities of life, which didn't amount to much.

Kentucky came to Casa Jim's only once a month or two to pick up his mail, which dwindled to just a trickle through the years, mostly from friends he met while traveling. He had no family; his parents had since died and he didn't know where his sister was living now in the states.

Jackson, after finishing the "character sketch" of Kentucky, walked out to the patio and saw Kentucky talking to a pretty blond girl from Denmark. Jackson thought that eventually Kentucky would try to get the girl to take a walk on the beach and try to put the make on her. Kentucky had told Jackson earlier that he often picked up a "bird" at Casa Jim's, usually the naïve and nymphs.

Jackson left for supper and then spent another hour in a local tavern before returning to Casa Jim's. When he entered he saw Kentucky passed-out on the bunk in the hallway.

The girl from Denmark and a fellow from England walked passed Kentucky on their way outside. Jackson overheard her:

"Kentucky's not much of a man," the girl commented to her companion in English. "In fact, he's not a man at all."

Nobodies

John and Tim were nobodies in their hometown of Birmingham, England. They were just average; in their early 20s, no steady girl friends, working at boring jobs and wherever they went they just blended in.

They never were popular enough to stand out in a crowd.

John didn't like it and he wanted to do something about it. Tim didn't like it either, and he usually let John make the decisions.

John decided to add some excitement to his life and also make lots of money. He signed up to become a mercenary in the uprisings in the Belgium Congo. Tim followed him there. With money and exciting stories to tell, the girls will take notice, John reasoned.

Tim returned home less than a year later. He doesn't talk about his experiences in the Congo, until he gets drunk and you can't shut him up.

Tim made fantastic money in Africa and he liked his job. He was lucky he hadn't seen too much action until one day he was told to go on a patrol with four other mercenaries.

With weapon in hand, Tim brought up the rear and the mercenaries carefully snaked their way through the jungle in search of the enemy. Tim suddenly heard something behind him so he whirled and fired his automatic weapon. A mother and two small children were there and he killed all three of them.

Tim tried to explain his actions to his fellow-soldiers but they just turned and continued their mission. That night, Tim couldn't sleep.

"A few days later, John died in action and medics drove Tim, who was under heavy sedation and devastated for losing his friend, to the hospital."

Today, Tim is still nobody in his hometown of Birmingham. He now is in his late 20s, has no steady girl friend, works at a boring job, and still isn't popular. He goes through life in a fog.

For Sale

I couldn't sleep last night because I worried about the government's lack of initiative to raise money for its pet projects.

I think Americans are taxed too much and the economy is bad and people don't want to spend lots of money on high profile things.

So, what's the government to do?

Sell the U.S. Army to corporate sponsors. I know the army is at war right now and I'm not making light of this but it is a known fact that the government doesn't know how to run any kind of business. Look at Social Security. It looks fine on paper but the government, as usual, screwed it up. If Microsoft or Wal-Mart ran their operations the way the free-spending federal government did, these companies would have gone bankrupt years ago. The only answer the government has, but private businesses don't, is to get more money by raising taxes to fund its projects. It would be laughable if Wal-Mart would tax every customer when they first walked through the doors.

I digress. Getting back to the Army. For a few million bucks, a company, say General Electric, can sponsor the 101st Airborne Division. Of course, the "Screaming Eagles" patches on the uniforms will have to go and be replaced by a picture of a light bulb. And when the soldiers jump over enemy territory they will be required to shout, "We bring Good Things to Life," which will be recorded in a television commercial for G.E.

A U.S. business won't have to buy a division. For lesser amounts, it can sponsor a company, a platoon or even a squad.

KFC's "The Colonel" will be the patch of "C" Company of the Second Battalion. For more money sent to the U.S. Treasury, "C" Company will be changed to "KFC Company." And, for even more money, KFC will be able to send its troops buckets of chicken. What a TV commercial that would make! Soldiers in fox holes chomping down on drumsticks and tossing the skeletal remains toward the enemy.

Krispy Kreme can sponsor "A" company, which will be changed to "KK" Company and tons of doughnuts would be shipped to the men of "KK."

And for "B" Company? Papa John Pizza. That will make that army unit "PJ" Company, which will be very popular for recruits. What 18-year-old wouldn't love to be someplace where he can eat pizza 24/7.

Soldiers of KFC, KK and PJ companies will have plenty of grub from their corporate sponsors. Pity the poor company that isn't sponsored and the men and women will be stuck with SOS (army slang for the ubiquitous creamed-chipped beef on toast) in their mess halls.

Huge U.S. businesses can spend billions of dollars and sponsor an entire war.

I can see it now. Katie Couric will announce on the evening news: "Heavy bombing again prevailed today at the terrorists in Saudi Arabia, a U.S. war brought to you by Budweiser..."

Barking Orders

"Today, gentlemen," the army platoon sergeant barked, "we're going on a search and destroy mission."

I looked at my buddy, Tony Boone, sitting next to me. He had a silly grin on his face, and he shrugged his shoulders as if to say, "ho-hum, look dogface, this is gonna be a snap."

I grinned back. Tony contends he is a direct descendent of the famed American mountain man Daniel Boone. Tony lives in Colorado and I hail from Arizona. This summer, we and about another thousand "officer-materials" were guests of the U.S. Army at Fort Lewis, Washington. All of us would be seniors in college this coming Fall, but now attending an ROTC basic summer camp for six weeks.

"It's about time we can go out and play killing people," I whispered. Little did it matter that the Army in its infinite wisdom didn't trust us with live ammunition for our M-1 rifles. My mind drifted and I actually turned off the sergeant's barking. I thought we would just have to attack an enemy stronghold and yell, "bang, bang, bang, you're dead." That's how we did it playing cowboys and Indians when I was way too young to be "officer-material."

"And squad D is the weapons squad," the barking somehow penetrated into my head.

Tony stirred; his grin disappeared. "Shit," he whispered. "We have to lug the heavy bazooka and 50-calibre machine guns while the other three squads get to attack the enemy with rifles."

Our squad got the short end of the deal on this dumb mission.

Somewhere on a huge battlefield encompassing rolling meadows, pastureland and wooded lots, a platoon of soldiers from another company wearing red armbands would be hiding in a dugout waiting for our platoon.

The three lucky squads would go out and hunt for them, but our squad would have to take up a position probably in a ravine and wait until one of the other squad leaders call on the two-way radio for heavy support from our bazookas and heavy machine-guns. We may have to carry the weapons for a mile and set up a firing line out of sight of the enemy.

After the sergeant's barking ended, our squad of eight lumbered to a ravine and dropped the heavy guns on the ground. We sat listening to the squawking of the lucky squad leaders:

"Red Dragon to Blue Sky, come in."

"This is Blue Sky."

"Protect us as we go over the ridge into the woods at 2 o'clock. Yellow Snake is going in on our flank."

The chatter continued for 45 minutes as the three squads ran all over the county looking for the hidden enemy.

Tony jabbed me in the ribs, and I grunted. "Hey, Don, do you know where Blue Sky is now?" he asked.

"Yeah, they're in the ravine by the water tank about a mile east of here."

"And Red Dragon is in the woods about 200 yards just north of them," said Tony, grinning. "Yellow Snake for some reason isn't answering the radio. They've probably wandered out of the county and are now on the outskirts of Seattle. Gimme that radio, will ya?"

I was the "very-bored-weapons-squad-leader-for-the-day" and without thinking I tossed the radio to Tony.

"Red Dragon, this is Yellow Snake, come in," Tony yelled into the two-way radio as he started to run away.

I jumped to my feet and began chasing him. "What are you doing," I screamed. "Give that back to me. We're not Yellow Snake, we're Purple Cow."

"Yellow Snake, where have you been?" I heard the radio squawked. Tony was at least 20 yards ahead of me. I stumbled and fell. Tony yelled in the radio: "We just spotted an enemy squad just 200 yards south of you in the ravine. Go attack them. We'll cover you and come in on your right flank and help you mop up.

I lay on the ground and began beating Mother Earth with my fists. "Tony," I cried, "the sergeant will kill us when he finds out what you did. He'll blame me for allowing you to use the radio."

Few minutes later, the Blue Sky squad leader yelled on the radio. Actually, he was cussing out the Red Dragon squad

leader for attacking him. We in the weapons squad thought it was kinda funny. I wasn't mad at Tony anymore.

An hour later, the entire platoon stood at a rigid attention in front of our barracks. The sergeant's face was beet-red, and he barked the loudest I have ever heard him before.

"We're goin' to be here 'til Doomsday until I find out which one of you clowns pulled that idiotic stunt on the radio this afternoon," he screamed, except he didn't use the words "clowns," "idiotic" and "stunt." "I'll have you covered with shoe polish because you will spit-shine everyone's boots in the platoon, and you also will spit-shine the latrine floor with a toothbrush, and…"

That's about the time Tony, who was standing at attention next to me, muffled a snicker. It just slipped out. The sergeant's face suddenly lost its redness, and for the first time in five weeks he actually smiled.

I couldn't sleep very well that night. Tony was making too much noise shining a mountain of boots next to my bunk.

Daniel Boone He Ain't

The busload of ROTC cadets, all cordially invited as guests of the United States Army to participate in summer training, bounced on the bumpy cow pasture someplace near Fort Lewis, Washington.

"Why do we have to go on this stupid night compass exercise," complained my seatmate. "It would be a lot easier to find our way in daylight."

"I don't know about you, Bud, but I've got it made tonight," I bragged. "I'm paired with Tony Boone."

"You lucky stiff," he muttered. "That means you two will be the first ones to finish and you can sleep on the bus while waiting for the rest of us to show up."

"Yep, you got that right," I said, leaning back in my seat with a silly grin on my face.

The bus skidded to a stop. A sliver of the moon hardly could be seen in the overcast sky. It was too dark for even shadows to come out tonight. We were in our fifth week of the six-week camp. Hundreds of Army ROTC cadets from throughout the western United States who will be seniors in college in the fall were at this camp. We were all future officers, but for six weeks we were treated as buck privates taking basic training.

The captain lined us up, gave us instructions and then sent us out two-by-two at one-minute intervals. When all of us cadets had disappeared in the darkness, he and the platoon sergeants would ride in the bus and wait for us at the pick-up point.

Tony Boone and I were the sixth team to leave. We were given a direction to follow on the compass for a specified number of yards. When we got to the exact spot, there would be a wooden post with a card on it with instructions giving us another compass reading so we could find the next post. (Note to reader: this happened many years ago before someone invented that fancy GPS gadget that can pinpoint and direct anyone to any designated square inch on earth.)

Tony and I would have to find several posts in this huge cow pasture dotted with bulky brush and stunted trees before finding the bus.

I let Tony read the compass and I marked off the paces. I knew we were in trouble after I walked the right number of yards in the direction Tony told me to and there was no post in sight.

"Are you sure you were reading that compass right?" I asked Tony. "I don't think any genes were passed down to you from your great-great-great whatever grandfather Daniel Boone."

"I read the compass right," Tony insisted, his voice rising slightly. "You klutz! You're the one who can't pace off an even yard."

We fanned out and in 10 minutes I found the post, about 50 yards northeast of where we thought it should have been.

"This time, I'll read the compass and you pace off the distance," I ordered Tony. He handed me the compass, and I followed the instructions on the post and pointed Tony on a west-northwest course for 358 yards. After 100 yards, I took the reading again and Tony was marching due north.

"You klutz," I hollered. "I'm reading this right, but

you're walking crooked. Isn't any of Daniel Boone's blood in you?"

"Shut up! You don't know the difference between a compass point and a pointless point."

"Huh!"

"Forget it."

Thirty minutes later, after fanning out again, we found the second post. This time Tony took the compass, and I paced off the distance.

For the next two hours, we were totally confused. We crisscrossed all over the huge cow pasture looking for posts. Once in a while we got lucky and found a post. Sometimes we even ran into other cadets, but they were always going in a different direction than we were. One time we ended back at a post we found an hour earlier.

"I hate to say this, but I think we're lost," I said. It was after 1 a.m. and neither one of us could find the last couple posts.

We sat down.

Tony shot up and swore. I smelled it. Tony had sat on a fresh cow pie.

In the distance two headlights blinked on and off. We looked at each other and we knew everyone was on the bus except us. The captain would undoubtedly have us clean the latrine with toothbrushes when we got back to the base.

"Tony," I asked. "Do you think it's very smart for a couple of ROTC cadets to go A.W.O.L. from summer camp?"

An Oven in my Jeep

My first day on the pizza-delivery job to earn extra money to get out of debt was a disaster. After finishing my day at the office, I quickly drove home in my new Thunderbird (well, it was one-year-old) and changed into some old clothes. Then I drove my big T-bird to the old pizza parlor and parked in front. The bossman assigned me to a dilapidated jeep with an oven inside to make my pizza runs.

I plugged in my oven to a wall socket near my jeep, and walked inside. Since I was new, the bossman gave me three pizzas, each in a cardboard box, and three addresses and told me to go and deliver them pronto. I noticed most of the regular pizza-haulers received about five deliveries at a time. I checked the addresses on the big map on the wall and walked out and put my pizzas in the oven.

I walked around the vehicle and unplugged the cord. I climbed back into my jeep. Smoke spewed from my oven. I opened the oven door and my three pizzas were on fire. I grabbed a rag, pulled my pizzas out and threw them on the ground. I stomped out the flames with my foot, and cheese, sausage, tomato sauce and mushrooms squirted up on my pants leg.

The bossman didn't scold me. He just gave me three new

pizzas but he instructed me to unplug the oven first before I put the pizzas in. "The red-hot coils in the oven shouldn't touch any part of the pizza boxes," he said. "You just learned what happens if it does."

I also learned to lower the top shelf in the oven so this wouldn't happen again. So much for my first day on the job.

I enjoyed my stint as a pizza deliveryman more than my bank teller job. I met all kinds of people, from the rich living in skyscraping apartment buildings in fancy neighborhoods to the hillbillies in uptown. Tips came in; I averaged a total $17 a night, although my highest was $23. (Remember, this was decades ago when gas cost less than 30 cents a gallon) The bossman only paid $5 for an eight-hour shift. The rest were made on tips, where the big money was. I worked an average of three nights a week.

There were a few things I picked up very quickly about being a pizza driver. You learned how to force a tip. When someone hands you a large note you change it, but you learn to fumble for the change – the last dollar or two. Most of the time they get the hint and say "forget it."

One night while waiting for the bossman to hand me five pizzas (I graduated to be one of his top deliverymen) another driver came up to me and told me he had just delivered a pizza where a young, attractive woman opened the door and she was stark naked.

"I damn near dropped my pizza," he said. "She asked, 'how much do I owe you.' I was hoping she would say, 'let's take it out in trade instead.'"

I saw many beautiful women when they opened their doors to accept their pizzas from me. Some were in slips, bathrobes, or negligees, but I never saw one naked nor was propositioned by any of them.

These jeeps were somewhat unpredictable. We always left the jeeps running while making a delivery to a house or in an apartment building. We had a chain with a lock on it to secure the door. Once I turned off the engine on the jeep while making a delivery and I couldn't get it started again. The battery died. Another driver had to come to pick up my pizzas and finish the deliveries. Another jeep towed me back to the pizza parlor. I was assigned another jeep.

Along with the pizzas, we also delivered sandwiches, ice cream, beer and liquor. After a while, you learn who the stiffs were. They are the ones who in the past didn't give you a tip. You recognize their names on the delivery slip. And some deliverymen punish them my giving bad service by putting them on the end of their run, mangling their sandwiches and "forgeting" to put their pizzas in the jeep's oven. The customer will bite into a cold pizza.

I, unfortunately, did this a couple times. One night I recognized a name of a guy who stiffed me the week before so I left out his pizza from the oven and even stuck the pint of ice cream he ordered in the oven for a while. That night, he gave me a tip. I really felt bad the rest of the night.

Some pizza drivers learn to make money in other ways, too. Before handing over any beer or liquor, we had to check the IDs of anyone who looked underage. We could have gotten in trouble if we sold liquor to minors. Some drivers took the risk and sold booze to minors but only for large tips – which they always set. Some drivers charged $10 or $20 on each delivery. The one time I did it I only put the price at $4. I sold a case of beer to a bunch of teenagers who were throwing a party in a house. The parents obviously were gone.

On reflection, some of the things I did to force a tip, or deliberately desecrate ice cream or a sandwich or gave out a cold pizza just to spite a "stiff" was really low. I knew I had higher standards, but in that period of my life, I succumbed easily to what my peers were doing.

I worked that job for several months and some of us pizza drivers got together after work to tip a few brews. We recalled those who were good tippers, exchanging names, and the weird people we met.

With my debts paid up, I quit that job. It was a bittersweet last day on the job. All the drivers and kitchen workers gathered as we shared a large pizza together – with a candle in the middle. I said goodbye, moved away and never been back to that Minneapolis pizza joint.

My pizza job was many years ago, and my doorbell just rang. The pizzaman is waiting with the pizza I ordered. I reach for my wallet. I'll give him a $5 tip. I wouldn't even think of stiffing him. He may deliver a pizza to me again someday.

Rambo, The Dog

Last Christmas, my older sister surprised me with an unusual gift – a needlepoint picture of a mournful, brown-eyed dog with big ears. Various hues proclaimed that "A Dog Loves You When No One Else Does."

I didn't tell my sister I've had dogs that spent sleepless nights plotting how to make my life miserable.

One of the worse was Rambo, a German Shepherd-mutt mix. Although lovable as a pup, he had a major flaw. He grew up.

In many ways, Rambo lived up to his movie-star namesake. He guarded our backyard with boisterous intensity. Woe to any stray cat, bug, bird or even a leaf that had the audacity to walk, crawl, fly or flutter on or near his turf.

If any one, such as the garbage man, ventured into the alley, Rambo would attack the six-foot cyclone fence desperately warning the enemy to go away. His ferocious barks echoed throughout the neighborhood. Perry Morse, my next-door neighbor, often complained that the barking interrupted his afternoon siesta.

My children, age 6 and 8, couldn't enjoy a few moments playing tag or swinging in the backyard. Rambo would jump on them or bump them. Bruised elbows and skinned knees were common, courtesy of Rambo.

"When are you going to find another home for that monster," complained my wife.

"He will settle down one of these days and will be a perfect house dog," I assured her.

"He better, or else you will be his new roommate in his doghouse."

One hot afternoon, I sipped iced tea on the patio and watched Macho Top Dog sneak behind a tree and freeze, waiting for anything from a frog to a housefly to come into view.

Then Green Beret Cutthroat would leap into action. I easily envisioned Rambo wearing two heavy bandoliers crammed with bullets hanging across his chest, a small steel helmet on his head and a bayonet in a sheath dangling from his hip.

One day, a woman wearing a green municipal uniform knocked on my door and said the weeds in the alley next to my fence were too tall.

"We received a complaint about the weeds and I'm writing you out a warning," she said. "You have five days to cut them down. You're violating a city ordinance, you know."

"I bet Perry Morse complained to you," I said. "I don't think the weeds are very tall at all. And why doesn't the city catch more burglars and not worry about my weeds?"

"I'll show you the weeds," she said, ignoring my question about the burglars.

In the backyard, I ordered Rambo to stay his distance and not bark. His lips curled a bit, and he crept to the tree and sat down. *Maybe he will turn out to be a house dog yet,* I thought.

"See those weeds? They're three-feet tall," the municipal woman pointed. "They've got to be cut." She looked around, and then smiled. I thought her face would crack.

"Hey, you've got a nice backyard," she said. "I love your petunias in the half-barrel."

She walked to the clumps of red, white and blue flowers, bent over and sniffed them.

Rambo sprung into action. Instead of being a Top Dog Green Beret Cutthroat he became a practicing proctologist sticking his nose where he shouldn't.

"Yeeooooooow!" the municipal woman screamed, straightening up.

Rambo quickly lifted a leg. One squirt, which hit her about knee-high, and then he disappeared around the corner of the house.

"You @*&%$?> dog," she screeched, waving her hands frantically after Rambo. She turned and looked at me. I tried to stifle a grin with my hand, and I could tell she felt sorry for me for having such an uncouth dog.

"You're obnoxious too!" she exploded. "I've had it! I'm giving you only 24 hours to clean up the weeds or you're paying a fine." She stomped back through the house to her car.

The next day, I chopped the weeds. I decided to celebrate by barbecuing a chicken on my small charcoal smoker. After placing a few legs and breasts on the grill, I remembered I left the barbecue sauce inside the house. Twenty seconds later, I returned and legs, breasts, grill and hot charcoal lie askew on the ground. Rambo was grinning; a chicken breast clenched in his mouth.

From that day, I barbecued on the front lawn. The neighbors chuckled, especially Perry Morse.

"Ha, Ha! Your dog kicked you out of the backyard again," he laughed as he walked by holding his well-mannered poodle on a pink leash.

"Hey, Perry," I said. "I know you like flowers, and I've got a bunch of new petunias in the backyard. You want to smell them?"

The Smile

It was a hot and humid August day in downtown Las Vegas. For some dumb reason I decided to dash across a busy street at mid-block to the comfort of my air-conditioned 1966 pickup, which is nearly 282,000 miles old.

An attractive woman in her 30s, driving a BMW, saw me and waved me across. As I walked in front of the shiny vehicle looking at her, she smiled.

Hey! Talk about an ego boost. I decided to smile back.

That's when I made the perplexing discovery: I was already smiling.

The lady drove on as I stood in the middle of the street pondering why I unconsciously walk around smiling.

HONK! A man in a little car glared at me. He wasn't smiling, although I caught myself smiling at him. This infuriated him more, and he cursed me as he drove by. I retreated to the curb.

As I walked along in the heat to my pickup, I recalled that lately a lot of strangers had smiled at me. Could it be I was smiling at them first? Or, do I have the kind of face people just smile at?

This was a serious problem. People wonder about people who walk around grinning for no apparent reason. I've even wondered about those people. Now I was one of them.

The next day, the same thing happened. Walking from my favorite restaurant in a casino, another woman I glanced at smiled at me. Again, I was smiling first.

Something strange was going on with my face, and I didn't know what. An hour later in the air-conditioned office, I corralled enough nerve to ask a co-worker if I walk around the office smiling.

"Are you kidding?" She burst out laughing. "If you smiled, your face would crack. I did hear you laugh once. I think it was in 1998 when you tried to say something funny."

I was making progress, though. I learned I don't walk around all the time smiling. At least not indoors. If something triggers my "smile" button, why doesn't it happen inside buildings?

A few days later, as the sun sliced near the western horizon, it happened again. A man smiled while walking passed me.

Whoa! Did I know him? No! I was smiling first. Why? I thought ... the man was approaching me ... I couldn't see him very well because of the bright sun ... so I had to...

I was squinting when I looked at the man. I hit the palm of my hand against my forehead. Ouch! Of course, I smile when I squint!

For several blocks, I tried it out. I squinted ... and the corners of my mouth turned up automatically. I squinted harder ... and my smile became broader.

I jumped into my pickup and headed to the nearest Wal-Mart. *From now on I will smile only when I want to,* I thought as I handed the cashier a $20 bill for a pair of sunglasses.

Daydreaming

Shortly after I became a teenager in the 1950s, I fell deeply in love with Marilyn Monroe. I would daydream about her, mostly while sitting at my desk in the eighth grade classroom.

Once in a while I would look around at the girls in my classroom and they were all either puny or chubby compared to my Perfect 10 first love.

Whenever I tried to reach into my mind and pluck out some nugget of truth such as the square root of 83 or who first circled the Cape of Good Hope, I instead saw her face and curvy body.

"Don," barked Mrs. Janowicz, my teacher. The picture of Marilyn clicked off, and I looked deep into the plump face of Mrs. Loudmouth Teacher, who was at my side bending over me. I couldn't help but get another closeup at the ugly wart on her left jaw with a couple of black hairs sticking out of it.

"Would you get your mind back on the topic at hand, namely Lewis and Clark," she scolded me.

"Yes Mam," I replied. "They discovered the Cape of Good Hope."

Mrs. Janowicz's face reddened and I think her wart even wiggled a bit and the two hairs crossed themselves as if to say "shame on you." The girls in the class snickered, and I hated them and I hoped someday they would see me with Marilyn at my side.

I hated them even more as I sat in the classroom alone (except for Mrs. Janowicz) after school. I had to write about the trek and discovery of the famed American Explorers Meriwether Lewis and George Rogers Clark. I also learned from a stern lecture Mrs. Janowicz gave me that the Cape of Good Hope wasn't even close geographically to the United States.

I think I was in love with Marilyn Monroe for about a month. I wrote her a letter and asked for an autographed picture. I hoped it was the one I heard about that made her famous. I never had seen the picture, but what I read in newspapers and magazines the nude photo must have been stunning.

After school, I would run to the mailbox and hope Marilyn's picture would arrive. But it never did, so instead I fell deeply in love with Janet Leigh.

I didn't even care if she was married to Tony Curtis at the time. It wasn't her fault that she hadn't met me. Someday, I would grow up and maybe I would have a chance to marry a movie star like Janet Leigh and I wouldn't have to sit with Mrs. Janowicz after school and take the ridicule from those puny and chubby girls.

Janet Leigh had class and looks, so I did what any "just-barely-turned-teenaged-boy" would do, write her a letter and ask

Janet Leigh (circa 1950s)

for a picture. That's what I did, and in about three weeks she sent me an autographed picture of herself. She was fully clothed, which, I guess, was okay with me.

I glued it to my wall underneath the picture of a boy sitting in a boat fishing with his grandfather. Whenever I barricaded myself in my room so my parents and sisters couldn't look in, I would remove the fishermen and dream about Janet.

"Don," my mother yelled. "This is the last time I'm calling you for dinner." I sighed, replacing boy and gramps on the wall and sauntering out to eat.

I was only in love with Janet for two or three months. That's when a new girl showed up in class. Nancy was a knockout and put all the other puny and chubby girls in the class to shame.

I discovered it was much better to stare at a lovely real person than dig deep into my mind and daydream about some photograph. I even paid more attention in class and raised my hand frequently to answer Mrs. Janowicz's questions. I could care less if I ever remembered what I had learned.

I just wanted to impress Nancy.

Blink

A pill box blinked at me yesterday.

This happened as I stood in front of several long rows of vitamin pills at Wal-Mart.

Yes, blinked…a flashing red light near the bottom of the box. It got my attention, just what the company that made the pills wanted.

I picked up the Flex-A-Min box. I learned this product "soothes achy joints," thanks to the glucosamine chondroitin pills inside. Underneath the box I read:

"This package incorporates an LED flashing light to bring attention (which it did) to Flex-A-Min special formulation. This battery operated mechanism is designed to operate for a limited time and may no longer be flashing at the time of purchase."

Is this a new trend? Companies coming up with new gimmicks to make me reach for a product on the shelf and put it in my shopping cart?

What's next? Minute Maid putting orange flashing lights on its cans of orange juice? Or red for its grape juice?

Companies don't have to use flashing lights to get people's attention. Why not talking products? Coke vending machines did it. How about Aunt Hattie telling you while walking by the bread shelves to "Be sure and grab my buns."

Or Peter Pan urging us: "Buy me, not Smuckers."

Why stop with flashing lights and talking products? You walk by the store's paint department and a can shoots you with a glob of harmless paint, the same stuff wannabe soldiers shoot at each other at weekend battles.

Or, walking by the movie DVD section and a hologram of a scantly-clan Halle Berry leaping out in the aisle in front of you purring…"Buy my movies…pleassssse!"

These companies may become shameless foisting all of this on the unsuspecting public in the future. But one thing for sure, I won't have any more achy joints.

How to Cuss

Newspaper reporters don't know how to cuss in print. They just plain lack creativity in the way they camouflage bad words.

Whenever they want to use a swear word in the family newspaper they use weird keyboard symbols such as #@*&$ and ~.

What does #@ and &$ really mean? When I was a newspaper reporter before I greedily took a buy-out, I spent countless hours in the newspaper's archives searching the newspapers for the last 27 years recording the weird cuss symbols in print. (Maybe that's why my boss offered me a buy-out?) After a thorough research on the placement of the symbols, I've concluded the way reporters use cuss symbols mean NOTHING AT ALL! One reporter spelled the famous "S" word using &(#$%^, while another spelled the same word %*@?#(. They are just plain inconsistent.

Wait a minute, alert readers are probably screaming now at me. Sure, there are other ways smutty journalists swear in print. I agree, but it is very uncreative by writing, "(expletive deleted)." Also, it is just too graphic and leaves nothing to the imagination by using the first letter of a swear word followed by dots for each of the other letters, such as "Q...." Remember, we are talking about a family newspaper and, by some strange chance, a teenager somewhere in the United States may sit down some day and actually read a newspaper.

After an exhaustive study of punching every conceivable combination of keys on my PC keyboard, I've come up with some symbols that get very little ink. How often have you seen these in your newspaper: [], \, ~, or ><? Not very often, if at all, I contend.

However, if a reporter really wants to get creative with potential cuss symbols, he could click on the multi-font wingdings or webdings. Look at these weird symbols we can cuss with: 🏛☎▸🏔🏕🏛👁🎿🏄🚶🎿 AA 👁✒🎸‖ ☈ ◀◀◁▸🚆.

After working until midnight couple nights a week for three months, I've come up with just the right arrangements of symbols to mean certain cuss words.

For starters, cussing by gamblers can look like this: $$$$$$$$$$$$$. Or if it is really dirty: **$$$$$$$$$$$$$$$$$$**. How about all you model railroad buffs out there: ###############.

Actually, reporters should not leave their readers too much in the dark. A three-letter swear word should begin with a "3." A four-letter word with a "4," and other words with "5, 6, 7," etc.

The next symbol should categorize the kind of swear word. I suggest a / ' for the crude obscene words; a @ for blasphemous utterings; a [] for gross bodily-function expressions, and a ?+ for words often used to describe our least favorite politicians.

The third symbol in a row will tell the degree of the bad word. Use a ****if you want the word to be full force. A half-hearted cuss word can be a **. After that, couple other symbols of the person's choosing can be thrown in for emphasis. My favorites are #!~ and (=>.

Thus, a gross bodily-function expression will look like this: 4[]****#!~. Or the hated politician: 8?+**%&/<.

Once and for all, this exhaustive thesis should be the standardize way to cuss symbolically in print. I hope a

Journalism 101 textbook company will include this story in its next edition.

Or, the publisher might just say this whole thing is a %(*@!?),< idea.

The Dilemma of the ZZZZZZ's

There's discrimination in the workplace!

I hear you: "**NO KIDDING, OSTRIDGEHEAD, YOU JUST WOKE UP AFTER SPENDING YOUR LIFE IN A CAVE?**" Except you used another word for "ostridgehead."

I'm not talking about the usual kinds of job discrimination. I'm well aware that women, Blacks, Hispanics and other minorities often have had a tough time climbing the corporate ladder. They keep getting bumped by a bunch of men wearing pin-striped suits and red power ties.

I discovered this fact shortly after I left college and landed an entry-level job. No matter how hard I looked, I couldn't even find the corporate ladder. The pin-stripers hid it from me. So, I settled down and decided to do what every true-blooded patriotic American does. I voluntarily give the first five months of paychecks each year to the federal, state and local governments. For this kind gesture, the government allows me to keep the rest of my year's paychecks.

I digress, getting back to discrimination. Why is it there are more women than men in the United States, but everyone consider women to be in the minority? But, that's not my point. What really ticks me off is men's and women's restrooms.

Every place I've worked the ladies' rooms come equipped with a little area for a sofa or couple of stuffed chairs. Women go there for a quiet place to sit, or even lie down. They relax before going out to bash their wits with the pinstripers.

We men don't have couches or overstuffed chairs in our restrooms. We need someplace to rest, too. Don't get me wrong, I'm not saying the pinstripers who also walk on entry-level men should remove the couches and chairs from the women's bathrooms. Women really need them. I know all about (well, maybe something) about women's biological clocks and their need for rest during certain periods of the month.

We men have needs, too. We have stresses and pressures and we would be more productive if we could relax and take a 5-minute snooze in our own restrooms.

I know this to be true because often after lunch I hide in my car in the company parking lot and take a "mini-vacation" siesta on company time. But when the weather is too hot or cold I have to work through the afternoon without taking a few Z's. I'm usually grumpy and there have been times I've fallen asleep at my desk.

I once asked my pinstriper boss why we men don't have chairs in our restrooms and he just laughed at me. That ticked me off even more. I'll fix him.

I hunted throughout the building for someplace to hide and relax and, EUREKA! I found it. The perfect place to nap – a bathroom stall. I sit fully clothed on the commode, my head cupped in my hands with elbows propped on my knees.

I had a hard time finding my stall. We have several men's rooms in the building and I tried them all. The one frequented mostly by the blue-collar men was too noisy and I couldn't sleep because I kept falling off the commode laughing at their jokes.

The restroom near the accountants and other desk-sitters was full most of the time and it took them forever to vacate a stall. The two-stall restroom on the top floor where the big bosses have their offices is perfect. These bosses always take a two-hour lunch break, leaving their little room empty over lunchtime.

However, I have a problem. One pinstriper, who brings his lunch to work, snores in the stall next to me.

The Valentine Dance

The father's 12-year-old daughter rolled her eyes when told he had signed up as a chaperone at her junior high school Valentine dance. She made him promise not to talk to her there or even acknowledge he even knew her. Daughter had a way to inflate his ego.

When Dad was her age, his extremely religious parents thought dances were sinful. He never went to a school dance. When he married, he and his wife decided that their kids wouldn't be so sheltered. He wanted to know what went on at a school dance. He personally didn't know.

The dance began at 7 p.m. Girls sat in clumps at tables on the east side of the cafeteria, and the boys stood awkwardly in groups on the west side. The DJ cranked up a song and the blast from the huge loudspeakers nearly swooshed Dad like a balloon against the wall. He retreated outside where a policeman stood.

"You're lucky," Dad told him. "You get to stay outside and protect your ears." He smiled.

The head chaperone appeared at the door and motioned Dad to come back inside. Dutifully, he did. The music was still deafening.

The head Chaperone screamed in his ear: "YOU JUST

CIRCULATE AROUND AND MAKE SURE NONE OF THE BOYS PUT THEIR HANDS ON ANY OF THE GIRLS' BUTTS. SINCE YOU ARE THE ONLY FATHER HERE YOU SHOULD CHECK THE BOYS' BATHROOM AND MAKE SURE NONE OF THE KIDS ARE SMOKING OR HORSING AROUND. ALSO, WALK AROUND AND MAKE SURE NO ONE CUSSES. WE WILL NOT ALLOW ANY PROFANITY."

"HOW CAN I HEAR ANYONE CUSS UNLESS I HAVE MY EAR AN INCH FROM THEIR MOUTH," he screamed back at her. "I CAN BARELY HEAR YOU AND YOUR MOUTH IS ONLY AN INCH AWAY."

"WHAT DID YOU SAY?" she yelled.

"NEVER MIND."

At 7:25 p.m., a few girls and boys had moved to the dance floor. They stood in groups according to their own gender. They hardly even looked at the opposite sex.

The DJ pleaded between ear-wreaking songs for the 75 junior-highers to dance. He played a slower – and softer – song to entice dancing. No one budged. But there was hope, some of the boys were actually looking at the girls, and the girls were glancing at them occasionally and giggling. The DJ gave up and the next song was a real head-basher.

Dad hurried to the bathroom and leaned against the wall next to the automatic hand-drying machine. The bathroom wall shielded him from some of the deafening noise. When he turned on the hand dryer, the humming drowned out more of the loud music. A boy walked into the bathroom and stared at the man whose head looked glued to the dryer.

Dad ventured out and saw some of the kids dancing. He quickly walked among them to make sure he didn't see any hands on butts. There was no way he could tell if anyone was cussing.

After about 40 minutes, 10 couples were dancing. (That meant about 50 students were still on the sideline.) Well, they really weren't dancing. The music was loud and fast and the boys had their hands on the small of the girls' backs, and the girls had their hands on the boys' shoulders. Their feet never moved an inch; they just swayed back and forth. Their bodies were at least a foot apart.

The music stopped, and the Valentine Day King, Queen, Prince and Princess were named. The girls screamed. When the two royal couples started to dance, the girls screamed louder.

Later, after returning to the dance floor from another bathroom visit, Dad saw the Prince dancing with Daughter. He liked him. He kept his hands on her waist and no lower. Dad sacrificed his ears for the duration of the dance and kept watching the smile on his daughter's face…and the Prince's hands.

Alas, after two hours, the dance – and loud music – was finally over. He walked the two blocks home alone. Daughter followed with friends at a safe distance. It wouldn't be cool for Daddy to walk Daughter home.

Later that night while watching television, Daughter sat next to him on the couch. He smiled at her. It now was cool for her to be with Dad.

Missed and Kiss

Missed

Missed him when he was born at the hospital.
Missed him when he took his first step.
Missed him when he bruised his knee.
Missed him when he scored the winning touchdown.
Missed him when he graduated from high school…and college.
Missed him when his grandson was born at the hospital.
And, finally, years later when the old man died, the son deliberately missed the funeral…and burial.

Kiss

A long time ago, a mother and a small child left their home and walked to the edge of a great cliff. Below them stretched a vast valley rich with much green vegetation. The world seemed to stand still as they looked.

The mother turned and asked her child if she would kiss her. "No mommy, not now," the child said. The mother leaned over and kissed the child on the cheek. They walked away together.

Years later the mother died, and the child, who had grown up to be in her 30s, went to the same spot at the edge of the cliff, as she did so many years ago.

Tears blurred her view of the green valley below.

Half-Century and Counting

In a few days, I'll be 50 years old. I've been waiting for depression to set in, but so far it hasn't. I got depressed twice before about my age, though. As it was for many others in my generation, age 40 was rough. About half of my expected life span was over and I wondered why every time I visited a local college I would see so many teeny-boppers.

I recall my first age-related depression. Actually, it was more like walking around shell-shocked. I was 18 and reading a newspaper. A beautiful woman in a bathing suit stared back at me. She had won a beauty contest and I could see why. The caption said she was only 18. WOW! That's my age, too! *Before, people who were physically blessed like her had been at least in their 20s,* I thought. Although she obviously had reached womanhood, I struggled for weeks with the fact that at age 18 I didn't feel I had reached manhood.

Now, nearly 50, and much older and wiser, it isn't mind-boggling at all that I already have crawled, toddled and walked on Earth for half a century. On the contrary: So far, it has been a blessing to be able to stick my toe in the waters of old age.

The American Association of Retired Persons (AARP) wrote me a few weeks ago, offering me a membership for only

$5. I joined, and now I will get Modern Maturity magazine, discounts at hotel and motel chains and home delivery of prescription medications.

My car-insurance salesman wrote to say that once I've reached 50, I'll be paying about $15 less a month on my insurance premiums. And, I now can live in Sun City retirement community and compete in the Senior Olympics.

"Down the road a ways, I learned at age 70 I'll be able to ski free at Sunrise Ski Resort in Arizona's White Mountains and get a free fishing and hunting license." And the ultimate: a letter from the President of the United States when I'm 80.

My grandparents got their letters when they reached 80 from President Reagan.

Maybe another ex-movie star will be president when I reach 80 and I'll get a letter from President Tom Cruise, or President Tom Hanks, or President Johnny Depp. Or – WOW!

From President Jessica Biel.

Refigure When Your Number's Up

Do you know when you will die of natural causes?

Providing an accident or major tragedy doesn't catch me first, I know exactly at what age the coffin lid will slam shut on me.

How do I know? I figured it out by reading the chapter, "How Long Will You Live?" in Marc McCutcheon's book, *The Compass in Your Nose and Other Astonishing Facts About Humans.*

(I'll digress to explain the book's title. All humans, apparently, have a trace amount of iron in their noses to help them find direction relative to the Earth's magnetic field. That way, people have the ability to use these magnetic deposits to orient themselves to within a few degrees of the North Pole, the way a compass does.)

That aside, the first step in the life-expectancy quiz is to start with the number 74. If you are male, subtract 2; if you are female, add 4. That knocked me down to die at age 72, but I added a year because I finished college (I would have another year if I earned a graduate or professional degree), and I added 5 years because I live with a spouse. Singles, according to the book, should subtract 1 year for every 10 years alone since age 25.

I was doing quite well until I was told to subtract 3 years because I work behind a desk. I'm at 75, now. I figure I'm generally happy most of the time, so I added a year, and I am between the ages of 50 and 70, so I added an additional 4 years. End of test, I'll live to age 80. That sucks!

More years can be added according to the book: if any grandparent lived to be 85 (add 2 more); if all four grandparents lived to be 80 (add 6); you live in a rural area with a population under 10,000 (add 2); if your work is physically demanding (add 3); if you exercise for at least 30 minutes three to five times a week (add 4); if you have an annual physical exam (add 2); and if you are between age 30 and 40 (add 2), 40 and 50 (add 3) and older than 70 (add 5).

On the minus side: subtract 3 years if any immediate relative under 50 has or had cancer or a heart condition or has had diabetes since childhood; subtract 2 if you earn more than $50,000 a year; subtract 4 years if you sleep more than 10 hours per night; subtract 3 if you are aggressive, tense or easily angered; subtract 7 years if you smoke a pack of cigarettes a day (8 if you smoke two packs or more a day); subtract 1 if you drink more than 1 ½ ounces of liquor a day; and subtract 2 years if you are overweight by 10 to 30 pounds (8 if overweight by 50 pounds or more).

So I decided to add at least 10 more years to my life. Let's see, I could easily exercise three to five times a week, increasing my age to 84. Because of my job, It would be difficult to add 2 years by moving to a rural area with a population less than 10,000. I hit a dead end at age 84 – 6 years shy of my goal. Nothing more could be added, I thought.

I read over the quiz two or three more times, and then it was obvious what I had to do to reach 90.

Women live an average of 6 years longer then men. I'll get a sex change.

It's either that or find a couple whose parents lived to be 80 to adopt me.

Part Two – People

Author's Note: I have been blessed in my more than 30 years as a newspaper reporter and working in corporate public relations to meet many interesting people and write about them in these companies' newspapers years ago.

I have used edited portions of these interviews on these pages to fit the format of this book. Some of these people who appear in the following pages have since died. I want to thank *The Arizona Republic, Milwaukee Journal* and International Minerals & Chemical Corporation for the opportunity to meet and write about these people.

The stories entitled *Things Not Going So Well, Hello My Friend* and *The Head-Hunter* were gathered during my 11-month tour of Europe in 1968, and reflect that era. Also, in Part Three – Places, *Dogology* and *Secluded Paradise* are based on my European trip. The edited and updated articles with different titles, *The Birthplace Visit* and *Jesus' Fishing Ministry*, originally appeared in *The Republic*.

The Head-Hunter

TORREMILONOS, Spain (1968) – Friends here call Loris Masini a "head-hunter," but hundreds of American women should take their hats off to him. He may have been the person who bought the human hair for their wigs.

Armed only with scissors and a fistful of pesetas, Loris combs tiny villages in southern Spain and tries to convince women to sell their long tresses.

"All these people are poor," Loris said. "And they haggle for every peseta they can get. You can't help feeling sorry for them; selling their hair means food and clothing for their families."

Loris, 66, a real estate agent turned "head-hunter," works for Giuseppe Iovino, a Torremolinos wigmaker.

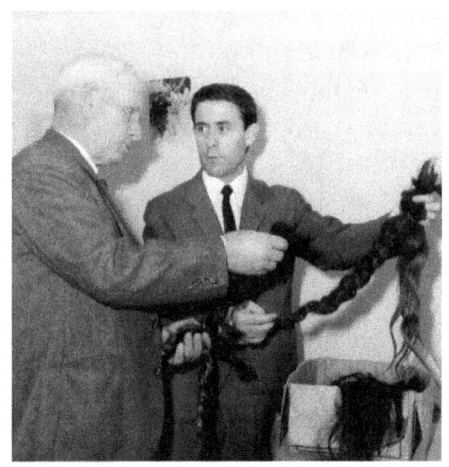

Loris Masini, left, and Giuseppe Iovino (circa 1960s)

123

Giuseppe pays him a commission for every pound of human hair he brings in. Last year, Loris carted 1,100 pounds of hair to his boss.

Most of the hair is made into wigs in Giuseppe's shop where the majority of sales come from stateside mail orders and American women vacationing here along Spain's Costa del Sol. The remainder of the hair is sold to other Spanish wig-makers who sell their wares mostly in the United States.

"When I first started this job two years ago, I was cheated all the time and lost money," Loris admitted. "Gypsies used to bring me long braids and I paid good prices for them. But, when we got the braids to the shop they were just short hairs woven together. It's hard to spot phony braids; even tugging on both ends won't always work."

The irony of it, he said, is that some of the hair came from Giuseppe's own shop.

"The Gypsies collected scraps of hair we swept out our shop and reshaped them into braids and sold them back to me," he said. "Now, we have to burn the hair scraps."

Loris pays Spanish women from $7 to $15 for their hair, depending on length, color and quality.

"The best hair comes from teenage girls because it is much softer," he said. "We prefer to buy light brown hair because it can be dyed either dark or blonde. Dark hair can't be dyed to a good quality blonde hair.

Girls making wigs (circa 1960s)

"I've made friends in many of the villages and they tell me who recently has cut her hair," he said. "Then I go to the home and try to bargain for it. But most of the time I pay one of the men in the village to go with me while I stop girls and women on the street. I have to get a villager everyone knows or else the women – and especially teenage girls – won't even talk to me as a stranger.

"If I get a teenager to agree to sell her hair, I also have to get her mother's permission. Sometime, that's where the real haggling begins and it may take hours before I can close the deal."

After Loris brings his haul to the wig-making shop, the hair is washed, bleached and dyed in the desired shade.

Nimble-fingered Spanish girls – there are eight of them in the shop – spend up to 30 hours hand-knotting a few strands of hair at a time until a wig is completed.

"There are two ways to make a wig," Loris explained. "Either machine-sewed or hand-knotted. A machine-sewed wig is faster and cheaper but produces a less natural-looking product that can only be combed in the direction the hair was sewn.

"The hand-knotted wig can take any kind of styling because the hair is tied to come straight out like natural hair instead of sewed flat."

Although Loris collects more than a half-ton of hair annually, he admits that times will be tough.

"In five years, it will be hard to buy hair in Spain," he said. "When the economy of a country rises, women just don't sell their hair. It used to be easy to buy hair in Italy, now it is difficult.

"I guess we head-hunters may be out of a job," he said, smiling.

Things Not Going So Well

The fat Czech woman sat behind the old tin-sounding piano and banged out a bad version of England's Engelbert Hmperdinck's popular *The Last Waltz*.

But hardly anyone in the Prague bar in August of 1968 listened. Czechs, old and young, sat behind long wooden tables and buzzed and laughed. The waiter ran with trays of beer.

The woman didn't care, she played louder. When she finished Waltz, she immediately swung into *I Can't Stop Loving You*.

I leaned back listening to her, my mind drifting. *I finally made it to Czechoslovakia,* I thought. *This will be a great vacation. What a happy people with their new-found freedom!*

I sat at a table with four Czech students who all told me they sought a democratic way of life, not communism.

"Drink, drink, drink," boomed one student on my right, raising his glass. We all raised our glasses.

"Cheers," and we all drank heavily. When we came up for air, we laughed.

Except Vladimir, the young Czech I met hours earlier at the train depot in East Berlin. We rode in the same compartment and talked all night on the way to Prague. I never talked to a Communist before. Theoretically, Vladimir was a Communist but he placed his new freedom above everything else. He seemed serious; I couldn't remember if I ever saw him laugh or smile.

Vladimir had saved his money and just finished a six-week vacation in Scandinavia. His three friends at the table had just come back after vacations in England. They could travel more easily now, and they saw much of the workings of the western countries. Pro-West-thinking Alexander Dubcek became first secretary of the country's Communist Party, replacing decades of hard-line Communist kingpins. The Russians disliked the freedoms Dubcek released on the Czechs and Slovaks.

"Things aren't going so well now in Czechoslovakia," Vladimir said to me above the noise in the tavern.

"What do you mean," I questioned him. "I don't know too much about communistic countries but I'd say the Czechs have it made now. Everyone is so happy, it certainly isn't like East Berlin. You can just sense the difference in the atmosphere between the sad people living in East Berlin compared to those in Prague."

"No, that's not what I mean," he shot back. "Dubcek's been making concessions to the Russians. He has to make more, I'm sure. One reason I was anxious to get back was to talk to people in the government. They don't like things that are happening now. Maybe the reforms are coming too fast."

Poor Vladimir, I thought. *He's too serious.*

"Drink, drink, drink," echoed my friend on the right, raising his glass. We all drank. Vladimir only took a sip.

Vladimir's friends didn't speak English as well as Vladimir did, but they were eager to talk to me.

One pointed to a young Czech soldier seated near us.

"Look at the metal design on his hat," he said.

I looked. It was a picture of a lion with two tails and a star over its head.

"Why does the lion have two tails," I asked.

"Because two people are here, the Czechs and Slovaks. But look at the star. There was a time when the star wasn't there."

"One of these days that star will be gone," I said boldly to my friends, not afraid to speak out anymore in Czechoslovakia. My friends smiled and we raised our glasses high and drank. Vladimir drank, but he didn't smile.

The next day, Vladimir showed me downtown Prague. He first took me to the main street Vaclavske Namesti. At one corner mostly college-agers gathered together in discussion groups.

"This is the free speech corner," Vladimir explained. "At one time we couldn't discuss openly. If we did, the police would come and break it up. Now they just walk around without bothering us."

We walked down the main street and I saw a large sign and started to laugh.

"Look at that," I said. "I never thought I would see something like that in a Communist country. Vladimir looked where I pointed. The sign, in English, read: "Heinz 57 Varieties" and it pictured a large can of Heinz soup.

"It's just like walking down an American street," I proclaimed. Vladimir didn't say anything.

We passed a store window advertising cartons of Camel cigarettes. On a wooden fence a poster advertised a movie, "Kleopatra" starring "Elizabeth Taylorova." I chuckled.

Vladimir led me down a side street and into a magazine store.

"Here, you can buy all kinds of foreign magazines and newspapers – *Life, Time* and the *International Herald Tribune*," he said. "We never could buy them before Dubcek took over. Sometimes a copy was smuggled in and passed around to us. Here, these copies are sold almost as fast as they are put out."

We walked past the Pan Am office – in the window were the Czech and United States flags side-by-side and a large portrait of President Johnson. In English, he extended to the Czech people "a most cordial welcome and sincere wish for a pleasurable and memorable visit" to the United States.

Then I remembered what one of Vladimir's friends said the night before. The only way the United States would let a Czech person visit the U.S. was if he had someone in the states to stay with. Then, of course, he had to declare enough money to get around.

Vladimir and I walked through an arch and into a courtyard lined with mod-art shops. A boy with long hair sat on the grass at the far end of the yard strumming his guitar and singing Bob Dylan's *Blowing in the Wind.*

"Very appropriate song to sing," I said, as Vladimir and I sat on the grass with about 25 other young people.

The singer got to the part "how many cannonballs must fly before they are ceased."

Vladimir muttered, "I wonder, I just wonder."

We stayed there almost an hour listening to a string of guitar singers, including many foreign young people visiting Prague.

Away from the courtyard we walked along the Vltava River past Charles Bridge, the famous old landmark of the city. Across the river stood Hradcany Castle, the presidential palace. As we walked, Vladimir pointed to a hill next to the castle.

"That's Letna Hill, and there used to be a large statue of Stalin on it, but it was taken down couple of years ago."

We walked on, and Vladimir pointed to a construction site.

"That's where an intercontinental American hotel is being built," he said.

"That's ironical," I said. "Stalin was taken down, and an American hotel going up."

Vladimir didn't answer and we walked in silence.

A few nights later, while Prague slept, Russia and four other eastern bloc countries moved into Czechoslovakia with tanks and troops. I went to Vladimir's home but he wasn't there and no one knew where he was. Some feared for his life.

Was he working in the resistance or had he fled the country?

The next day I crossed the border into Austria on the special train taking foreigners out, and I thought of Vladimir. I hoped he was safe. He was a serious person, and I understood now for the first time why he never smiled or laughed the short time I knew him.

Dr. Robert Blanchar with boom-machine

Cannon in the Cornfield

The white pickup bounced to a stop beside the test plot near Libertyville, Illinois, and Dr. Robert W. Blanchar and I climbed out.

We walked to a strange looking metal object about two feet high with a six-inch barrel between the rows of corn.

"That... is for the birds," said my companion.

BOOM!

"It's pretty loud," I shouted against the cannon's echo.

"It's effective, too," Dr. Blanchar replied. "And not a bird gets killed. This is a personal battle between me and those blackbirds. Last year I won."

Dr. Blanchar is a research agronomist at a large agricultural company headquartered in Illinois. He oversees several acres of corn test plots.

Just before the cannon went off again, Dr. Blanchar explained how he came by the newfangled piece of equipment.

"Each year thousands of blackbirds flock in from nearby nesting areas and attack the young corn ears," he said.

"The raids could ruin an entire test plot, so we had to come up with some way to keep the birds away.

"Scarecrows were totally ineffective. I can even walk..."

BOOM!

"...down the rows and wave my arms and those birds won't move."

His remarks, between cannon blasts, were getting hard to hear.

He said something about coming up with the answer last year when he placed two cannons midst the rows of corn.

"The cannons don't shoot anything, and we can regulate them to make loud booms as often as we want," Dr. Blanchar said...I think. Between other booms, I understood him to say that one cannon can keep birds away from two acres of cropland.

"How does it work?" I asked.

BOOOOOOM!

"...tank...carbide..."

"What did you say?" I asked.

Dr. Blanchar shook his head, took my notebook and drew a diagram. It showed that:

Water drips from a tank on top of each cannon into a container of calcium carbide powder, forming an acetylene gas.

Next, a timing spring sets off a flint striker, causing a spark.

Then, the acetylene ignites the oxygen of the air, causing the loud boom. There is little if any smoke.

I took the notebook and we walked back to the pickup

truck. It was then that Dr. Blanchar coined a phrase that I actually could hear:

"A quart of water and a pound of calcium carbide a day keep the blackbirds away."

And me!

Hayseed Hick or Savvy Entrepreneur

ERICK, Oklahoma – No one warned me of Harley Russell, so I was ill-prepared for his boisterous off-beat sarcasm.

I'm not alone. A reporter for *The Oklahoman* newspaper once noted Harley and his wife have "scared more than their fair share of folks."

But stick it out. The two of them are really fuzzy, teddy bears in grizzly clothing. Their persona is strictly shtick, an unusual way to entertain you.

It was by chance my wife and I entered the old city meat market in the hick hamlet of Erick, just off I-40 near the Texas-Oklahoma border.

A "Roger Miller Museum" sign attracted us to drive into Erick. The outward appearance of the museum in an old building was uninviting, but another building a block away caught our eye. The façade featured decaying "Texaco," "S&H," "Coca-Cola," "Greyhound" and "Route 66 Roadside Attraction" signs.

Another sign on the old brick building bragged: "Welcome to Erick, Oklahoma. The Redneck Capitol (sic) of the World! Yee Haw! See Rednecks work and play in their own environment!" Another sign: "Insanity at its finest."

We climbed out of our car and stood in the middle of the vacant road (there is hardly any traffic in downtown Erick) snapping pictures. A slender woman with long, silky gray hair wearing blue overalls pedaled up, parked her bicycle and unlocked the door. "Come on in," she greeted us.

We walked in and crates of soda pop were stacked inside the door. I didn't know what kind of place this was – a grocery store, antique store or maybe even a museum?

Antique signs were everywhere, along with old lamps, record albums, chairs, electric fans, garden tools, guitars, books, china cabinets filled with trinkets, posters, board games and photographs.

"Is this an antique store?" I asked.

"No," a voice behind us resounded.

We turned.

A grizzly-looking, barefooted man with long hair and shaggy beard wearing blue overalls with no shirt smiled at us. A front tooth was missing.

Harley began his shtick pitch. Nothing in the place was for sale. A museum? Not hardly, he never would run one. He scoffed at Erick's two home-grown celebrities – Roger Miller and Sheb Wooley.

He asked how we found the place. We told him the Roger Miller Museum sign on the freeway caught our attention and we wanted to check it out but we didn't. We said we had a picnic with our two dogs in the town park instead.

Harley laughed, and accused me of smoking marijuana in the park. He said my wife looked like a Baptist minister.

We were ready to walk out. Harley then dropped the shtick for a moment. The truth came out.

The place is a curiosity shop, and the woman who let us in was his wife, Annabelle. They offered us something to drink – lemonade, ice tea, pop? We declined.

Annabelle handed us a stack of newspaper clippings, a picture of the couple taken 20 years earlier when they first opened the shop, and a picture post card Annabelle had sketched of the storefront.

We learned from this material that Harley grew up in Erick. At age 12, Roger Miller gave him a guitar and at that young age Harley began singing in local honky-tonks.

After graduating from high school, he left Oklahoma and spent 22 years on the road playing back-up guitar to such stars as Charley Pride, Jim Ed Brown, Dottie West, Jan Howard and Dave Dudley. He hit bottom after three failed marriages, smoking dope and drinking liquor.

He returned to Erick to settle down and get his head cleared. He bought the brick building, the former city meat market with a tin ceiling and scuffed wooden floor, for $2,500. He went into business: a guitar shop, a game room and an antique shop. All these ventures failed.

In 1987, Annabelle, a California resident, came to Oklahoma to visit her grandparents. She walked into Harley's shop one day to have her guitar tuned. Within days, they fell in love and later were married.

Business was slow through the years and they had plenty of time strumming their guitars and singing alone in their shop, which was only a block from the famed Route 66.

In 1999, a man walked in while they were strumming and said he drove a tour bus and was ahead of schedule to stop at a restaurant. He asked if the tourists, all from England, could come in and look around.

Harley and Annabelle continued to strum and sing and at the end of a song the tourists began clapping and throwing money on a nearby table.

When the travelers headed back to the bus, the driver asked the couple if he could bring in another tour group in a couple of weeks. "Would the Russells entertain them? How much would they charge to fix some sandwiches so the tourists could stay longer the next time?"

"I said, 'We'll do it for free,'" Harley said.

Since then, an average of more than 40 tour groups annually stop at their "Sandhills Curiousity (sic) Shop" for a free show and a free lunch. Harley and Annabelle never ask for a dime, but there are some tip jars sitting on tables.

"When we tried to do it as a business, it didn't work," Annabelle said. "When we quit trying to do it as a business and just entertained them for free, it worked."

Word spread of the new venture. (Type "Harley and Annabelle" on the Google search engine and see what pops up) A friend brought 1,500 Harley-Davidson motorcyclists who were on a trip along Route 66 to the shop.

The couple has appeared on television in Norway, France and Australia. French tourists show homemade movies on the Russells on the internet. The couple has appeared in various Route 66 magazines.

Pixar visited them while doing research for the movie *Cars*, and it modeled a location in the movie after their shop. The two were reportedly part of a composite for Mater, whom Larry the Cable Guy lent his voice to in the movie.

Harley and Annabelle were invited to the *Cars* premiere in Charlotte, North Carolina. They declined, although they signed releases giving Pixar permission to use in whatever way it wants their likeness, names, faces, voices and curiosity shop.

The couple also was invited to the pre-screening of the movie in Oklahoma City and asked to perform in the Governor's Mansion. Again, they declined.

Harley said he shuns the "celebrity" status but would rather stay in Erick to entertain old and new friends.

"We've finally gotten to where we like it," Harley said. "Now that all Route 66ers are coming by and we've got these tour groups, I wouldn't have a shop in San Francisco if it was given to me and paid for."

The Russells have found their niche. They live frugally; she has a part-time job in a motel. They have taken an unusual tact to win friends. And they have fun doing it.

After 20 minutes chatting with the couple with a few more insults thrown in, and examining the old odds and ends sardined inside, we left.

The couple invited us back. They posted the hours of their curiosity shop:

"We open when we wake up, and close when we pass out!"

Harley and Annabelle Russell

Curiosity Shop storefront

Hello, My Friend

Americans living on a shoestring hitchhiking across Europe and North Africa become callous to pushers. Tangiers has the most of them.

We already learned to say, "bug off," especially to those who accost us with, "Hello, my friend. Are you fine? Want some hash…kief?"

"Bug off, bug off," we respond.

We walk through the Medina, the old, vice-infested quarter of the city, and sit on the sandy beach and gaze across the blue Atlantic.

A voice looms behind us. "Hello, my friend." We didn't turn to look.

"Bug off."

"Oh, you are rude. I have good deal for you."

"Bug off, we're not interested." I turned. A small boy in tattered knee-length shorts and dirty legs stood there.

"I suppose you want a free handout. Bug off."

You want to buy some kief…hash…anything? I can even get you a girl."

"How old are you," I ask.

"Eleven."

"Your parents know you're doing this?"

"My father taught me. You come to my room and I show you stuff. It's real good. Come."

"You know English pretty good. How many languages do you know?"

"French, Spanish, German, Italian and Portuguese. Do you want to buy…"

"No, bug off kid. Bug off!"

George Burns

When George Burns was 88, he was still traveling the country putting on shows. He even appeared in movies while in his 80s. As a newspaper reporter with *The Arizona Republic*, his publicist wanted to know if I wanted to interview him. My editor agreed.

"Sure," I said. "When do I fly to Hollywood."

My editor frowned. "Use the telephone at your desk," she said.

Crap, I thought. Chained to my desk again.

I dialed. Someone said Burns would be right with me. I took a deep breath. G-e-o-r-g-e B-u-r-n-s, I really hit the big time; I wish I could meet him personally, though.

"Hello," the voice came through the earpiece.

I exhaled, said some dumb greeting and plowed into my first question.

"Are you smoking a cigar right now," I said, thinking what a dumb first question to ask a major Hollywood star.

"Right now," says Burns.

"Do you have...

"You bet."

How many cigars do you go through in a day?

"Oh, maybe 15."

145

(The interviewer is beginning to feel like the straight man in a vaudeville comedy act).

About 15?

"Yes. Well, at my age, if I don't hold onto something I might fall down."

At an age when most entertainers are content to rock quietly in the shade, Burns still travels and performs before packed audiences. His movie, *Oh, God III,* came out when Burns was 88. The movie is about a kid who sells his soul, an action that leads to a showdown between God and the devil, Burns says, adding, "And, of course, God wins. I always win. I play God and the devil. I play both parts. I think it's a very good movie. I love movies anyway, because when you're on the stage you gotta stand up for an hour. When you're making movies, you can sit down and act. At my age, if I can sit down and get paid it's nice."

How does it feel to portray God? *(Another dumb question. I hate interviewers who ask the "how do you feel" questions. Now, I are one. Crap, again)*

"Well, when I play God I don't use makeup."

Have you heard much criticism?

"No, in fact the churches kinda like my God. It's an honest God. It's a God that's very human, makes a few mistakes."

Will there be an *Oh, God IV*?

"Well, if *Oh, God III* makes money, I'll come down again."

Burns' lofty status in show business is undisputed. In a *People* magazine readers' poll in 1980, he tied with Bob Hope as "favorite well-known older American." One difference was discernible among the voters: Women preferred Burns to Hope.

That brings up another Burns trademark, which made me ask the cigar question. Since the 1920s, when he teamed with his now deceased wife, Gracie Allen, Burns rarely has been sighted without a cigar in his hand. Nowadays, in pictures of him holding a cigar, he is frequently surrounded by attractive, much younger women. Would he consider marrying again?

He says he is too old to marry a second time.

Although Burns pokes fun at his age, I learned there is also a serious side.

"I'm not interested in what I did yesterday," Burns says. "I'm only interested in where I'm going tomorrow, what I'm doing today."

What's the source of his spark?

"Your audience gives you the vitality. I love what I'm doing. If you love what you're doing, you can do it all your life. It's something to get out of bed for. If you stay in bed, it doesn't work. Bed is no place for a guy my age. I can't make money in bed.

"I'm making old age fashionable," he adds. "You don't have to get old. You can't help getting older, but you don't have to get old."

Do you have any advice for people who are thinking about living to 88 and beyond?

"Not to retire," he says. "Do something. Have a part-time job, be charitable. Do charitable work. Do something. Get out of bed."

I got off the phone thinking I was richly blessed with the opportunity to interview Mr. Burns. And now, years later, I recall that in 1996 I was saddened to hear that Burns had died at age 100. And seven years later, the other popular old-timer, Bob Hope, had passed away. He also was 100.

People magazine has to find some more famous American old-timers.

Two Sides of Pearl Harbor

On that Sunday morning when the island exploded, a scared 19-year-old soldier crouched behind a machine gun. From his perch on top of a 60-foot tower, Charles W. Blazek was ordered to fire at the enemy – Japanese bombers and fighters that were attacking Pearl Harbor.

In the air leading the attack on the Hawaiian island was Mitsuo Fuchida, a captain in the Imperial Japanese Navy Air Service. He had 361 airplanes under his command. When the attack ended, two United States battleships, a minelayer and two destroyers were either sunk or damaged beyond repair. A total of 188 U.S. aircraft were destroyed, and 2,388 people were killed and another 1,178 were wounded.

Fuchida returned to his Japanese aircraft carrier triumphant and a war hero. Even Emperor Hirohito summoned Fuchida for an audience.

Blazek, however, was shaken for days.

"I don't believe there was an enlisted man who didn't expect the attack," recalled Blazek some 20 years after the onset. "The way things were buttoned down and the guard doubled, we knew that something was going to happen."

Blazek was a member of the 62nd ordnance company. Three months earlier, it had been ordered to move the eight-inch guns from a carrier into shore batteries on hills overlooking the bay.

When the attack came, Blazek, of Milwaukee, said, "I was so scared that I was mentally numb. It took two days before I realized what had happened.

"Some of the planes came so close that I could have spit on them. I know I raked several planes from the front to the back as they flew overhead. I heard some of them sputter, but I don't know if they went down."

Blazek may have hit Fuchida's plane. When the commander returned to his aircraft carrier, he found 20 large anti-aircraft holes and the main control wire was barely held together by a thread.

Blazek went through the war island-hopping in the Pacific, coming out as a master sergeant. Some 20 years after the war, Blazek was appointed to organize the Wisconsin chapter of the Pearl Harbor Survivors' association. At the time, he was the only one from Wisconsin although nationwide there were 10,000 members.

Meanwhile, Fuchida's life after the war changed dramatically. In fact, he even came to American shores as a Christian missionary.

But that's getting ahead of this story. After Japan's defeat, Fuchida went through a period of depression. His hope for the Japanese empire expanding throughout the Pacific was crushed.

An American missionary handed him gospel literature on the street a few years after the war. Fuchida read the message written by an American airman who was in a Japanese prison camp during the war. The airman related how he once hated the Japanese people, but after his conversion, he loved them.

Fuchida read the tract and it inspired him to buy a Bible.

While thumbing through its pages, he read how Jesus Christ, while hanging on the cross, forgave those who were crucifying Him.

With this assurance of the greatness of Jesus' love, Fuchida, too, forgave his enemies and was converted.

In 1952, Fuchida was asked to become the chief of staff of the reorganized Japanese air force. He told his superiors to give the position to one of his friends.

"For me, I'll never come again with bombs but with Bibles; never a soldier of hate and war, but a soldier of love and peace in Christ," he said.

Five years later, Japanese Premier Nobusuke Kishi offered Fuchica the minister of defense position. Fuchida refused, and asked if another man could have the job.

"I'll spend the rest of my life trying to encourage my people to adopt the Christian way of life," he told the premier.

He authored a book, *From Pearl Harbor to Calvary*, and also was featured in *Reader's Digest*.

He made missionary trips to the United States.

"I believe the Lord permitted me to be the Pearl Harbor leader so I can now lead many of my Japanese people to the Lord and the Christian way of life," he said. "When I speak under the title 'From Pearl Harbor to Calvary,' many who would not come to hear other Christian pastors or missionaries speak, would come to hear me, having remembrance of Pearl Harbor."

Thirty-one years after the war, on May 3, 1976, Mitsuo Fuchida died at age 73 in Kashiwara, near Osaka.

People on the Move

Across America from the 1960s to the present, these are the people I met who I thought had interesting jobs, hobbies, an unusual outlook on life or they did something strange or weird.

Consider Walter Durlak, printing ink specialist at the Stresen-Reuter plant in Bensenville, Illinois.

We find Durlak leaning back in his swivel chair opening a copy of *Playboy Magazine*.

He displayed the center foldout—a full-color picture of The Playmate of the Month, a shapely astrologer's assistant wearing a revealing, sheer negligee.

"We had a lot to do with this page," Walter told his visitor. "Notice the skin tones. Nice job of printing, isn't it?"

Walter explained that among his company's products are basic chemicals for printing ink used by many magazines, including *Playboy*.

"In this case, one chemical binds the pigments within the ink, another makes the ink dry faster, and a third helps create a protective finish so the image can't be scratched or smeared off," he said.

I forgot to ask him if he just noticed the great pigments and protective finish in the centerfold, or did he actually looked at the study matter at hand?

• • •

In just 25 seconds, Bette Mitchell whiffed her way through a six-course dinner.

The meal was unusual. It was neither filling nor, by the usual standards, a gastronomical delight. As a matter of fact, it was "thrown together" in just a few minutes.

Her meal consisted of pulling several of the 1,000 bottled food odors in International Minerals & Chemical Corporation's Food and Flavor Center in Skokie, Illinois.

First she had a quick sniff of sherry, followed by a hors d'oeuvre course of cheeses (blue and cheddar) and figs. Then came whiffs of an orange, some vegetable juice and soup.

Before trying the more substantial main dishes, Bette turned up her nose at cider champagne.

Then she rapidly sampled bottles of pizza (with pepperoni), ham, potatoes, and bread and butter. For dessert she inhaled deeply of early-season watermelon and cantaloupe. The meal was "rinsed" down with several sniffs of coffee.

The best part of the "meal," Bette said, was she didn't consume a single calorie.

• • •

One cold morning Mathew Neilon picked up a 30/30 level-action rifle and headed into a feldspar mine deep in the mountains 15 miles from Buckingham, Quebec, Canada.

Inside, he aimed and fired up into the huge rock dome more than 200 feet overhead. An icicle crashed down.

"If we let icicles get too large, they'll fall – and could seriously hurt someone," he said. "I shoot them down first."

Neilon, the mine foreman, does his shooting early in the morning before anyone else comes to work.

"It may sound like a funny way to get rid of icicles," he said, "but we've found it's the only practical way without shutting down the mine and using scaling methods."

Neilon, who joined International Minerals and Chemical

Corporation in 1950 after spending many years working gold mines in northern Canada, said winter temperatures drop to 30 degrees below zero in the Buckingham mine.

"We have to wear a number of trousers and sweaters to keep warm this time of year," he said. "I even wear my long underwear in the summer.

• • •

Jack Baggett's car is his office—and also often his lodgings for the night. Officially, he works out of warehouses in Alice and Hebbronville, Texas, when he is not on his job as a drilling mud engineer in a state as big as all of two outdoors.

"The last time I had to sleep in the car was for four nights straight," said Baggett, grinning. "Even so, I almost got fat on the job."

Baggett explains that the occasion was a wild week in which oilmen were fighting a runaway oil well, with thousands of pounds of subterranean pressure boiling gas up the drill pipe.

Baggett concentrated on taming the gas by shooting enough of the right kind of drilling mud down the drill hole to plug up the formation through which the gas was escaping.

"The well was out in the country, and I couldn't leave, the situation was so critical," he recalled. "So I just slept in the car. But one of the oil rig's crew fixed up a big barbecue pit, and truck drivers hauled in food. That's how I almost got fat on the job."

• • •

As the wildfire began peeking above a nearby mountain, the residents of Vallecito, Colorado began packing for the just-ordered evacuation. Shirley and Ray Robinette and their grown children and spouses, operators of the Buffalo Gap Restaurant, were ready to leave. The grown children left, but

Shirley and Ray just turned around and unpacked.

"We tricked our children," said Shirley, "we decided to stay and stick it out."

As the flames crept closer, Shirley and Ray hunkered down. Firefighters appeared and that's when the couple rolled up their sleeves, fired up their restaurant stove and started cooking for the 2,500 firefighters on the scene. They fed them for free, not charging them a penny.

"We just stocked the freezer with $7,000 worth of food," Shirley said. After a few days the food began to run out. The couple contacted McDonald's and Burger King for food. They both agreed to donate food for the cause. McDonald's came through, but Burger King, Shirley said, charged them $180. "Burger King went back on their word," Shirley said.

The smoke was so heavy the couple had to sleep on the floor, where the smoke just wasn't as thick. The fire destroyed 12 buildings and burned the hillsides on two sides of nearby Vallecito Lake. "God left, and the devil moved in," Shirley said.

The Buffalo Gap Restaurant, which displays 150 stuffed animals including a cape buffalo and the third largest mountain ram ever shot, was spared. The fire jumped over the building. Shirley believes that if she hadn't stayed the restaurant would have burned down. She believes God rewarded them for staying and feeding the firefighters.

However, there was a price to pay. Shirley let herself become dehydrated, and she was taken to the hospital. A couple days later, her husband who has diabetes and heart problems, became stressed and was admitted in the hospital, too.

• • •

Juraj Slavik, a member of St. Patrick's Episcopal Church in Washington D.C., manned a booth for the St. Francis Burial Society at the general convention of the Episcopal Church in Minneapolis, Minnesota in 1976.

She pointed to a pine box, a coffin. The 200-member burial

society, she explained, was founded three years earlier after the death of Jenny Moore, wife of the Rt. Rev. Paul Moore, bishop of the Episcopal Diocese of New York.

Jenny wanted to be buried in a pine box but it was difficult to find anyone who made pine coffins. After a search, a woodworker in Rockville, Maryland, was found who could supply pine coffins.

The traditional, hexagon-shaped coffin sold for $185. For an extra $15, shelves and a wine rack would be added to the coffin. "It's great to have it for intermediate use," Slavik said, adding that the society also sells a cardboard coffin for $10 for those who want to be cremated.

• • •

Durward Staten Jr. pushes brooms for a living. No, he isn't a professional street-cleaner or a janitor; he's a master broom maker in Mountain View, Ark. He sells brooms in booths at arts and crafts shows across the United States.

"There are only about 20 to 30 of us in the nation who are actually master broom makers," Staten said. "It is a dying art. We only copy early-American brooms...that were made by the pioneers in the early 1700s and 1800s."

He explained that the bristles come from broomcorn, a plant that is grown specifically for making brooms.

"Primarily, we get ours from Mexico, which furnishes about 95 percent of the broomcorn used in the world today," Staten said, adding that the plant resembles corn (although it is in the sorghum family) and 40 to 50 long fibers grow from the flower head. The fibers are used for the broom bristles.

"It would probably take somewhere from 50 to 60 stalks to make one broom," he said. He uses sassafras limbs for the wooden handles.

Staten makes a concession, though. Instead of using a leather strip or rope to bind the bristles as the pioneers did, he cheats by using wire.

• • •

Jacky Alling, the box office manager at the Sundome Center in Sun City West, Arizona, takes on extra roles as a matchmaker and peacemaker.

Years ago, two elderly women walked up to Alling and bought tickets for an upcoming concert dance.

"Could you seat us next to two nice men?" one of them asked.

Later that day, "two nice men" stood before Alling asking for tickets to the same concert. With a smile and a glint in her eye, Alling put them next to the women.

Not everything is "peaches and cream" for Alling. There are times people show up with tickets years after an event. These ticket holders, who bought tickets but missed a performer's earlier Sundome appearance, try to get in the second time around. One time, a man who only had one leg and his tiny wife wanted to get into a show on just one ticket.

After one show, a man complained to Alling that he had sat on something hard during the entire show and he wanted his money back. He showed her a set of false teeth someone had left on his seat.

• • •

Peter J. Hill is one of about a half-dozen people in the Metropolitan Phoenix, Arizona area making a living by working full-time in community theater. He acts, sings and dances, but most of the time he directs plays and musicals.

One period of eight weeks he was involved in six productions simultaneously.

"They all opened in a course of six weeks," Hill said, shaking his head and vowing to avoid that madness again. During this time his average day went like this: Wake up, go to a morning rehearsal and then head for other rehearsals at 1, 3, 6 and 8 p.m.

Did he ever consider leaving Phoenix, which isn't really

a theater-going town, for Los Angeles or New York City? His answer: No!

"I would rather be a big fish in a little pond," he said.

• • •

George Lane, of Sedona, Arizona calls himself the sloppiest painter in town. He refuses to clean up his act because his paint-splattered works sell. "At 67 or 68, I started painting seriously like this—if you call it serious," said Lane, gesturing at his drip-lined canvases hanging in a local gallery.

He uses elements of both impressionism and abstractionism in his acrylic works. The colors are bright and the images, many of them curving, reflect energy and motion.

Lane has dabbled on canvases and paper most of his life. In 1931, a friend got him a job as an apprentice in Walt Disney's studio. Five years later, the head of the makeup department at MGM saw some of his sketches of movie stars and lured him away. For 40 years, Lane was a makeup artist for such stars as Spencer Tracy, Clark Gable, Tyrone Power, Elizabeth Taylor, Jean Harlow, Greta Garbo, Joan Crawford and Katharine Hepburn. When Jean Harlow died, Lane was summoned to make her up before the line formed to view her in the casket.

He retired in 1976 and moved to Palm Springs, California. "I wasn't doing much of anything," Lane said. "I unpacked everything and sat there and said, 'What in the hell am I going to do?'"

He taught art at a school for retarded children and during those two years his mind became freer and he began to paint. People saw his sloppy work and began buying his paintings. They sold for at least $1,000 each in the 1980s.

"When my wife plays bridge, I paint,' Lane said, chuckling. "I don't use oils anymore; I might not be around by the time they finally dry."

• • •

Len Agrella, an artist, paints animal skulls in bright colors. He also create paintings and sculptures. He painted a shipping crate in bright colors and it will end up as a very expensive room divider.

Agrella, of Prescott, Arizona, uses color to transcribe the feelings or personalities of the animals into human feelings.

"You get 10 cow skulls together and they all look the same," he said. "But if you start painting them, they start to take on different personalities. Each one will tell you eventually how it should be painted...should it be blues, or blacks or browns or reds? I'll just grab something (a paint color) and try it on."

On the day of this interview, Agrella stood near a red and hot-pink steer skull with grafted, color-matching deer antlers. He titled the $2,500 piece *Mating Out of Your Species*.

He produced a small painting about half the size of a post card that is a self-portrait. People question him how long it took to draw it and are amazed that he asks $1,000 for five minutes of work.

"What they fail to realize it took me 35 years and five minutes," Agrella said, adding people often would comment that their kid could do that.

"They probably could," Agrella said. "Children probably do the best art in the world, but then their minds get sophisticated and it ruins them. You have to de-evolve."

Agrella thinks he has "de-elolved." He produced a series depicting women breaking out of cocoons.

"It's only within recent years that I realized everybody doesn't look at stuff like I do," he said. "That's why they buy my works."

• • •

Gunther Gebel-Williams reinvented the art of lion-leopard-tiger training. There was a time when the circus animal trainer would enter a cage full of ferocious lions and tigers, armed with a chair, whip and a pistol loaded with blanks.

The animals would roar and take swipes at the trainer as he fended off sharp-clawed paws with the chair. People would gasp but secretly loved the threat of violence and blood.

Gunther, instead, establishes a rapport with the animals that they become docile. At least, that is the way it appears to the audience.

However his arms and hands show many scars made by animal teeth and claws.

"I only have two whips and my command," he said. "It looks so easy today; many people think the animals are on dope. But they have claws and teeth; I could make them very wild in seconds.

I must be ready for anything, I take nothing for granted. The trick is to make it look easy, but the truth is that it is a constant struggle."

Most of his injuries were suffered while breaking up fights between animals. Once, a leopard leaped at him, going for his throat. Gunther threw up an arm for protection, and it was ripped.

He doesn't lord over his cats, but instead tries to become their friend. "Animals cannot be trained with a whip and intimidation. I use a system of rewards for a job well done. Each animal is different, just like people. Some learn more easily than others. I have to take each one and work with it personally. I must find the right animal for each trick. For some I must be tough, and for others I must be gentle and encouraging.

"I spend 15 hours a day with them. I feed them and clean them and take care of them," said Gunther in an interview in 1983. He later retired from the ring, and he died in 2001 at age 67.

• • •

Olaf Wieghorst, a Western artist who died in 1988, painted from his mind, not from photographs. He has Will Rogers to thank for that.

Early in his career as a budding artist, Wieghorst, who at the time was with the New York City Police Department mounted patrol, met Rogers. He gave the famed cowboy a sketch of horses standing in snow in front of a saloon.

Rogers told him it was a nice drawing, but since the horses were there for a long time there should be some droppings.

Wieghorst said he took the sketch home and painted some droppings and brought it back to Rogers a few nights later. Rogers looked at it and said that since there was snow on the ground it probably was cold.

"Yeah, I suppose it is," Wieghorst told Rogers. "And he said, "Why the hell isn't it steaming?" He really taught me something about being realistic.

Wieghorst, born in 1899 in Denmark, would devour dime novels about Buffalo Bill and other cowboys as a boy. As World War I neared its end, Wieghorst got a job as a cabin boy on a ship and worked his way to America. At age 19, he enlisted in the U. S. cavalry and was sent to Texas. Later, he worked as a cowboy on ranches in Arizona and New Mexico. Then he became a mounted police officer in New York City. He retired in 1944, and at age 45 moved to San Diego determined to become a full-time artist.

And more than 40 years later he was considered one of the top Western artists of his time. He sold two companion paintings on Navajo Indians for nearly $1.5 million. A Wieghorst original may sell for hundreds of thousands of dollars. Collectors of his works through the years included presidents Dwight Eisenhower, Gerald Ford and Ronald Reagan and actor John Wayne.

• • •

Linda Lee Curtis used to paint on canvases and carved sculptures. Now, however, she has pushed the canvases and clay aside and applied her brush to potato chips.

Why?

"Nobody else does it," said Curtis, who has painted sunsets, faces, designs and trees in bright acrylic colors on potato chips. She pokes holes in some to make earrings and necklaces.

Through trial and error, she has perfected her chip art. She has learned that Pringle chips are the best ones to paint. "There aren't as many bubbles," she said.

Curtis uses a paper towel to scrub the salt and grease off each chip. She has concocted a secret formula she applies to the chips to harden them. Then she spends three to four hours painting each chip. She also has a market painting scenes on lima beans.

"I'm going to work with ripple chips," she said. "Fritos and cheese curls are next."

• • •

Harry Blackstone, world-famous illusionist, was on the phone:

"I'm looking for a volunteer to be cut in half. Are you busy?" Blackstone asks. He uses a buzz saw on people in his cutup act.

"Well, ah, I don't know. If you clue me in on how it's done…

"You don't have to know how it's done. You don't do it – I do," Blackstone says.

"In other words, I'll have 100 percent faith in you?"

"That's right. Interestingly enough, I did this just a couple of weeks ago with a reporter in Toledo who is now working in Cleveland and Cincinnati."

As impressive that act, the showstopper is when he removes a glowing bulb from a lamp and it stays illuminated. He lets go, and the bulb floats in the air and into the audience. People handle it, and then it floats back to the magician.

"That's the one that has been my bread and butter," Blackstone says.

The magician sums up his business: "The skill we have is totally a learned technique. Certainly, you or any 10-year-old child could do what I do – with 15 years practice. (A magician) makes you as the audience believe what you are seeing is real, when in fact it is all fantasy."

Blackstone revealed he has another trick that involves levitating a person and letting him float out into the audience, then up to the ceiling. While the person is in full view, he disappears.

There is silence for a moment on the phone. I'm just glad he didn't ask me to volunteer for that, too.

• • •

Swanee Huotari picked up his divining rod and walked onto my property, 3 1/3 acres of desert southwest of Phoenix.

Within 10 minutes the rod jerked up and down. Huotari counted the jerks. When they stopped, he smiled and turned to me.

"There's gold down there about 12 feet," he said.

Huotari's hobby is unusual, and according to the retired ironworker, only a few people will succeed at it. He's a dowser, a person who claims he can find underground water, oil or minerals by use of various divining rods, ranging from a forked branch or a bent piece of wire attached to a metal rod that sells for $400. He uses them all. Some people say the use of a divining rod is the work of the devil, but Huotari cites articles that state there is evidence that the mysterious work of dowsers could be related to their sensitivity to the electric forces emitted by underground liquids or minerals.

Swanee Huotari (circa 1980s)

He found the gold on my property using his $400 rod. First, he placed a vial of water in the compartment and held it over the spot on the ground. It didn't move.

He took the vial out and put in a gold wire. He explains that this rod won't work unless it has a sample of a liquid or mineral in it that is the same as the underground substance.

The rod containing the gold sample went wild when Huotari held it on my desert lot. He walked around my property and within 15 minutes found water at 34 feet at three different spots, indicating an apparent underground stream.

Gold and water were on my mind when we drove back to Phoenix. I planned to borrow someone's backhoe and dig for the gold.

But then Huotari burst my bubble. He explained that his $400 divining rod can pick up mere specks of minerals. It is possible my gold is really placer gold, or flakes mixed in the rocks and sand.

Then I found out something else about Huotari's $400 divining rod. It can't determine the difference between real gold and fool's gold.

• • •

Paul Guisinger and his helper, Harlie Banfill, are the only workers on the graveyard shift at International Minerals & Chemical Corporation's feldspar and silica plant in Kingman, a town in northwest Arizona.

"Our main job at night is to make sure the mills continue to turn out product," Paul explains. "Practically all of the maintenance, repairs and heavier work are done during the day."

Paul says his night duties include being a watchman, although he's "never had any trouble with vandals or other unwanted guests.

"Part of the job on the graveyard shift is checking the separators that send the finished product to the bins or divert coarse ore for regrinding.

"Since feldspar and silica are ground to a powder, they have a tendency to pack. I sometimes have to unclog the pipes, particularly when it rains or there's dampness in the air."

He says the ore comes from nearby mines.

As Paul walked throughout the plant checking machinery, Harlie led the way up ladders to the top of the huge storage tanks above the plant. The lights of Kingman on the sprawling plateau could be seen for miles along the snake-like highway.

"Pretty sight, isn't it?" Harlie asks.

Shortly after 4 a.m., the two men fill the mills with flint rocks the size of a man's fist. The flints roll in the churning mills, crushing the feldspar and silica ore into powder. Feldspar is used in ceramics, glassware, plumbing fixtures, foam rubber matting and even false teeth. Most silica is used in the manufacture of detergents and scouring powder.

So, when some of you take out your false teeth at night and drop them into glasses of water, Paul and Harlie may have had a hand making them.

• • •

The Milwaukee ballroom in the mid-1960s was packed with hundreds of Seribian-Americans seated around dining tables. Their eyes darted anxiously at the swinging doors.

Then a man entered.

Even before most of the diners could get to their feet a thunderous applause erupted. Above it all shouts were heard:

"Long live the King! Long live Peter!"

Petrushka Karageorgeovitch, 39, walked to the head table. He was known to the crowd as King Peter II, former monarch of Yugoslavia who fled his country from the Nazis in 1941. He had been living in exile ever since.

People in the ballroom stared at him: would he order the chicken or the beef? Is he right or left handed? Even when one of the speakers said something humorous, they glanced to see if Peter was laughing. Much of the time he was. The rest of the time he smiled.

"He's a symbol of our country," one man said. "The king is not only the glory of the past but the determination of the present and the freedom of the future," said another.

Later, in an interview, he was asked if there was any chance he would return to Yugoslavia?

"I sincerely hope so," he said. "I have kept in touch there all of the time and have many sources of information."

But it never happened to this forgotten king. Years later when communism was driven out, the country split and new countries popped up. A war developed and the United States military was pulled in.

The people didn't want a kingdom. Petrushka Karageorgeovitch was never invited back. In fact, he never saw the fall of communism. He died in 1970.

• • •

Chen Dan Qing, an artist from the People's Republic of China, hopes to chart new innovations for the staid Chinese art.

"It is too bad that in the Cultural Revolution (1966-76) China closed the door, closed the eye and closed the mind," Qing said. "That's terrible for us. We never have seen the West's original works in Chinese museums. Since the revolution, we didn't know what is comtemporary, modern art in the West and international. We artists are very traditional and very classical. We want to know the modern arts."

Qing attended an art institute in Peking, and later moved to New York City to learn modern art, especially oil-painting techniques. Since Qing moved to New York, other Chinese artists have followed, and they have formed a close community. Several of them visited Arizona to visit museums and art galleries.

"We see here (the Southwest) the art is realism, more traditional technical style," he said. "Subject matter is Indian people in everyday life. In New York, if you see some realism style, it is not necessarily of people's life. The subject matter is more of an idea, not a lifestyle."

Unlike many American artists, Qing said he will shun painting Indians. He believes he has to live with the people and absorb their lifestyle before he can portray them on canvas.

The art market in China is almost nil. There are no art galleries, and the government pays artists a salary. Once in a while, the government sends art works out of the country for sale.

Qing said most Chinese are more concerned about necessities of life than putting something decorative on their walls.

"During the last few years, there has been more freedom to paint landscapes, portraits, everyday life, still life and some nudes of models," he said. "The government lets people show that work and collects it for the national museum. But, I never think I can sell art (there)."

Note: Now he can. There has been a turn-around in the Chinese art market since Qing was interviewed in the 1980s. "It is no secret that the Chinese contemporary art market is blistering hot..." *Forbes*, April 7, 2008.

People Who Inspire

People who knew Carol Moore years ago were nice to her because they feared if they weren't, Moore would cause them to have a migraine headache, or worse.

"I made no bones about it," she said. "I was a witch. I wore a tattoo of Satan on my right hand."

Moore talked openly about a phase of her life before she accepted Jesus Christ as her savior when she worshiped Satan and believed she could cast spells, using knowledge picked up from occult magazines.

On two occasions, she said, she corralled demoniac forces to do her bidding far beyond the headache stage.

Once, Moore said, a young woman said she was pregnant. The woman didn't want the baby and didn't want an abortion.

Moore said she called upon demoniac forces through a Satanic ritual. Three days later, the woman had a miscarriage.

"I in no way touched her physically," Moore said.

Another time, Moore cast a spell at 8 p.m. one night to inflict severe injury on a woman she hated. Early the next morning, the woman was seriously hurt in an automobile accident, which had an effect on her for years.

"This weighs heavily on my heart," Moore said, adding

that she is sure the supernatural powers she called up caused the accident.

Now, as a Christian, she tells others of her conversion and her experiences in the occult and warning them about what she calls the satanic powers behind such so called "harmless, little games" as ouija boards, tarot cards, crystal balls and white magic.

• • •

For several years, A.L. "Archie" Doughty, would sit in a chair outside Food City Super Market in south Phoenix passing out gospel literature.

Also, as was his daily custom, at 6 a.m., Doughty would knock on the door of an ailing widow who lived in his apartment building to walk the woman's dog.

Doughty, a widower and retired auto mechanic, told his friend and pastor, the Rev. James Hiatt, that "he was a rotten rascal or something like that and that he wanted to work the rest of his life for the Lord."

And so he decided to be a missionary and a friend to the wayward, elderly and sick. He went weekly to Library Park, a rest spot for drifters and drunks, and preached using a small public address system.

However, the city made him stop. But, Doughty would visit several rest homes and nursing homes in south Phoenix to conduct Bible studies.

"He passed out about 3,000 to 4,000 gospel tracts a month, mostly at Food City," the pastor said. "I don't know how he kept up with everything. Sometimes he would forget what day it was and not come to church. He was...always busy, checking people and being nice to people"

Although Doughty brought cheer into lives of others, he had his own health problems of late – diabetes, heart trouble, poor circulation in a leg, and hospitalization for a ruptured appendix.

One day, people at Food City didn't see Doughty, 81, although his chair and a box of tracts were there for shoppers to help themselves. A sign, prepared by a friend, explained that the Lord had called the old man "home." Doughty had died earlier that morning.

• • •

Evangelist Billy Graham sat in a small room across from a newspaper reporter in 1974.

"If I had my druthers, I would rather be a pastor in a small church somewhere and go through all the human experiences that people have," he said. "I think I miss this…marrying…burying…being with people in their joys and sorrows. Although I have a great deal of it, it is nothing like a clergyman or pastor of a church."

Graham has preached the gospel throughout the world to millions and millions of people. In 1973, the largest number of persons ever assembled for any event in South Korea – more than a million – squeezed together on a large field

Billy Graham (cicra 1970s)

to get a glimpse of Graham and to hear his message, which was translated into the Korean language.

Graham held two crusades in Arizona. He said that even before he arrives in town his evangelistic team had been working in the area for months preparing people to work behind the scenes. Graham emphasized that all the prayer that goes on before he starts a crusade already works to create positive results in people. He said he could just stand up and without preaching give an invitation and people would flock to the front. The Holy Spirit, through the prayers of believers, was working in the hearts of people even before the actual crusade started.

Graham said in his 1974 Arizona crusade that unless moral and spiritual values are restored in every area of society, "the free way of life we have known in the free world will not survive."

"…I believe that one of the problems in the world today that is not recognized is the great intensification and acceleration of evil in the world…because the devil knows his time is short.

"The coming of the Lord Jesus Christ may be drawing near. The kidnappings, the violence, the terror all over the world I believe are part of a demonic activity."

Although decades have passed since Graham uttered these comments, his prophesy is truer now than before.

• • •

James Marsh, a 1961 graduate of Arizona State University, stepped out of America's affluent life and moved in with the Stone Age people of Western Australia.

When he first arrived at Jigalong village, the desert home of some aborigines, the people were camped away from the village in a dry creek bed under trees. It was cooler there than on the sun-scorched desert.

While unloading his gear from a pickup, an old man wanted to know how the white stranger was related to him.

The aborigine tribe later determined how Marsh was related to some members of the tribe – he was given parents, sisters, brothers, grandparents and cousins. Even potential wives were selected.

"To them, people are more important than things," Marsh said.

Marsh, a Wycliffe Bible translator, said after reading in Life magazine about the aborigines in Western Australia, he was convinced he should go there to translate the Scriptures in their language. He lived with the tribe three years before he was fluent in their language.

"That was when I could carry on a conversation and laugh at the jokes," he said. "It took another two years before I felt comfortable enough to start translating..."

"They don't have the word 'love' in their language," Marsh said. "But while I was learning the language and I heard the word 'stomach,' I felt it might have to do with emotions.

"The stomach is similar to the 'heart' in English. The way you say 'I love you,' is, 'you are sitting in my stomach.'"

He said when he translated the 10 Commandments he had another problem with the last commandment, "Thou shalt not covet thy neighbor's...wife...."

"The words for 'covet' are 'swallow spit,'" Marsh said, adding that many people, when they desire something, suck in air, which causes swallowing.

In that context, the commandment was written, "You shall not swallow spit for another man's wife."

• • •

"When I was eight, my mother told me, 'I don't love you, you are the son of the devil.' This hurt me and I hated my mother...I was brought up in a life of witchcraft," said Nicky Cruz.

At 15, Cruz moved to New York City from Puerto Rico and became a member of the 225-member Mau Mau gang in the Spanish Ghetto.

"New York City was a jungle and the law of the jungle is like living like an animal," he said. "I behaved like an animal. I was in a tough neighborhood and people were being killed each day."

Once, a rival gang member beat him and shot him in the leg. Cruz was hospitalized for two weeks. He got revenge. He hunted the youth who injured him and hit and kicked him so severely that he was in the hospital for three months.

Another time, Cruz jumped a policeman and was arrested. A court-appointed psychologist concluded, telling Cruz, "You are the worst. There is no human power that can help you."

But there was. David Wilkerson, a country preacher, came to the ghetto and started to preach on the street.

"He (Wilkerson) said there is a God-power who can change you." Cruz didn't believe him. The next time Cruz saw Wilkerson the preacher stretched out his hand and said, "Nicky, I want to be your friend."

Cruz said he hit Wilkerson in the face, bloodying his nose. Cruz quoted Wilkerson: "Nicky, I came here to tell you that Jesus loves you."

Those words haunted him, Cruz said. Later, Cruz and some of his gang members attended Wilkerson's crusade meeting. It was there that Cruz and about 20 of his gang cried as they accepted Jesus Christ as their personal savior."

• • •

Mrs. Alta Garcia, 60, never has seen a tree or a flower or even the face of the man she married 21 years ago. She was born blind.

Yet, through the years, Mrs. Garcia of Nogales, Arizona has taught a Sunday school class for sighted children and has taught numerous blind people in Nogales to "see" by teaching them Braille.

She also has encouraged hundreds of other blind people in the United States, Latin America and Africa to walk a spiritual life by preparing, and sending them, Braille Christian literature free of charge.

"One elderly lady in Southern Mexico who was 82 received some of the literature and accepted the Lord" Mrs. Garcia said. "I get a lot of letters from people who said the literature has helped them to grow and walk in the Lord."

"When I was young I wanted to be a missionary and I was willing to go anywhere to serve the Lord," said Mrs. Garcia one afternoon in the 1970s in her three-room apartment behind the Mexican Baptist Church. She helped found the church 30 years earlier with a missionary couple.

Mrs. Garcia graduated from the Arizona School for the Deaf and Blind in Tucson. She applied to two mission boards; one didn't answer her, and the other turned her down because she was blind. "After that, people told me that I would never make it on my own."

How wrong people can be.

• • •

Naomi Sautter is a missionary on an Indian Reservation in southern Arizona, but once in a while she can be found in Tucson bars.

"Bartenders don't know what to make of me," chuckled Mrs. Sauter, a white-haired widow who at first glance looks as though she should instead be at home with grandchildren on her lap.

After entering a bar and eying the patrons, the white woman might walk to an Indian man and scold him, "Come on, we are going home."

Then she escorts him home to the reservation where his family awaits him.

"If you're going to be a missionary you have to put pride in your pocket and not worry what people think or say. Some (Indians) like me and some don't. There are no in-betweens among the Indians."

Mrs. Sautter never intended to become a missionary, but

once while attending a missionary conference, she was challenged to serve on the Papago (Tohono O'odham) reservation. Her parents and brothers disapproved. Mrs. Sautter lived in a miner's shack, with rattlesnakes sometimes being found under the bed, refrigerator and sink. Someone told her to get Siamese cats; "I hated cats...but I'd rather have cats than rattlesnakes in the house."

A lynx she named Oscar lived on her roof. She threw bones on her roof for Oscar. The lynx and the missionary lived together peacefully thereafter.

She is the founder of Quijotoa Community Church, about 60 miles south of Casa Grande, on the 8,100-square-mile reservation where 15,000 Indians live in 96 villages. Her ministry is based on faith since she is not affiliated with any denonination or mission board.

● ● ●

For more than 25 years Mark Fenney-Davis said he killed people for a living. "Now, I'm a servant to men," he said.

He works at the Phoenix Lighthouse Rescue Mission in Phoenix, washing sheets that alcoholics slept on the night before and mopping the dining room floor where derelicts spilled soup and dropped bread crumbs. It was there months earlier that Feeney-Davis, who speaks with a stiff British accent, was down to $3 in his pocket. He went to the rescue mission for financial help, but instead found God and received "a complete peace that I never had in 25 years."

Feeney-Davis served with England's Special Air Services during World War II and parachuted behind enemy lines. A fellow lieutenant was tortured and killed and Feeney-Davis said he became an "absolute, vicious killer."

Later, his parents, who were plantation owners in Kenya, were brutally murdered by the Mau Mau, his mother repeatedly raped and his father disemboweled. "My motive was revenge."

Feeney-Davis joined a special group of about 50 ex-soldiers to fight the Mau Mau.

"It was all hand-to-hand combat," he said. "When we captured a Mau Mau we tortured him to get information. They did the same with us."

When the terrorizing ended in Kenya, Fenney-Davis returned home, married, but became restless. "I missed the killing and hunting instinct," he said.

He got mercenary jobs in Arabia, the Congo, Burundi, Biafra and other places. His wife pleaded with him to quit and stay on the plantation. When he didn't, she committed suicide.

"In effect," Fenney-Davis said, "I killed her. I didn't fight for any political cause. It was strictly for money.

"If I was fighting for one side and the other side offered me more money, I would switch sides and kill those who once fought with me."

In Biafra, he was shot, and a Baptist missionary found him near death and pulled him into a nearby mission station. He fought the urge to surrender his life to Christ. "I was afraid. It takes guts to be a Christian. It doesn't take guts to kill people."

After two years spending money gambling and on women all over the world, he landed on the Phoenix mission doorstep. It was in the mission he asked God for forgiveness.

"I have an element of peace now," Feeney-Davis said. "It is like a child who has come home."

• • •

Manuel Arenas picked up the sewing needle and walked to a wooden idol sitting on a shelf in the jungle hut deep in the eastern Mexico mountains.

If I stick this needle into its foot and blood comes out, I'll know my mother is right, Arenas remembers thinking. *If it doesn't, I will know Don Pedro is right and I will follow his God.*

The Totonac Indian lad, about 12, plunged the needle into the foot. The needle snapped into pieces and there was no blood.

Arenas said that incident caused him to turn his back on the pagan religion and accept Christianity, which he learned from "Don Pedro" (Herman Aschmann), a Wycliffe Bible translator working in the Totonac tribe.

After his conversion, Arenas' father disowned him. He was forced to leave home and he went to live with the Aschmanns. He helped the missionary translate the New Testament into the Totonac language.

Determined to get an education, he went to schools in Mexico City, Dallas and at the University of Chicago. He earned a master's degree from the University of Erlangen in Germany.

During this time he learned English, Spanish, French, German and Italian fluently. He was offered high-paying jobs because of his language skills but he chose to return to the Totonac nation and open a Bible school that trains Totonacs to read, write and preach. Also at the center is a church, a clinic that handles 80 to 100 patients daily, a farm where students raise livestock and grow corn, beans, bananas and oranges, and facilities

Manuel Arenas (circa 1960s)

to record radio programs that are broadcast throughout the Totonac area.

For 24 years before Arenas died in 1992, the peasant-turned-preacher trained his people to step into a world of Christian love, not idol fears.

• • •

Jane Russell was a popular pinup girl during World War II, and in 1943, her first movie, *The Outlaw*, was censored because of her plunging necklines. (My, how times have changed)

"I thought it was ridiculous," Russell said during a telephone interview in 1984.

Compared to the daring scenes in today's movies, how does she view her revelations in *The Outlaw*?

"That looked like Little Bo Peep," she said. "It was mainly just a publicity campaign, and I think they (the movie moguls) were doing that on purpose. Got to stir up a little. They even enjoyed the fact it couldn't pass the censors."

Russell went from plunging necklines in *The Outlaw* to perform in 23 movies, make commercials for Playtex, perform in television shows and team up with Connie Haines and Beryl Davis, all members of the Hollywood Christian Group, to perform concerts across the land. Their rendition of the spiritual *Do Lord* sold over a million copies. "We were the first ones to ever have a spiritual on a pop label," Russell said.

Russell, who had a back-alley abortion that messed her up so much that she couldn't have children, adopted three children while married to Bob Waterfield. In the 1950s she founded an organization to help locate permanent homes for children classified as unadoptable. Also, following her belief in Jesus Christ, she formed the Hollywood Christian Group and opened her home for Bible studies.

Does she think about acting once again?

"Oh, I don't want to do it unless it's...something with a message," she said. "I think America's on the upswing, and we're trying to build, get our character back. I'd really like to do a modern-day religious film."

• • •

A Phoenix hospital janitor has developed a therapy program to cheer up patients while he is mopping floors and cleaning the bathrooms.

It's a smile, a wave, a friendly greeting, the singing of a song or the composing of a poem for a patient.

Clarence Reed knows what it means to suffer and carry a heavy burden. He was hospitalized for a year from a World War II injury that left the right side of his face paralyzed. His ankles are stiff and he limps when he walks. When Reed leaves his job each day, his responsibilities are far from over. His invalid wife is bedridden. Each night he gets up three or four times to take care of her. Reed has a 16-year-old daughter who has cerebral palsy and is confined to a wheelchair.

Reed gives God credit for strength to work during the day and care for his wife at night, although he admits that it could become almost unbearable.

It is not uncommon for Reed to stop by the pediatric section of the hospital and visit the children. He buys them stuffed toys and, when nurses approve, gives the children candy and gum. Sometimes he will sing a funny song about "My dear old daddy's whiskers."

Once, a 17-year-old boy was dying of kidney failure. His parents wanted their son's last days to be happy. Reed befriended the boy and talked to him about Jesus Christ. He also talked to the boy's parents daily. When the boy died, Reed wrote the eulogy at the funeral.

One day, Reed was mopping the floor and walked past the bed of a patient who had met Reed in the hospital three years earlier.

"Ol' Clarence, you still here?" the man called to Reed. "I feel better already just seeing you, Clarence. Don't forget to drop by, sing me a song, tell me the latest news."

Sometimes Reed will kiss a terminal patient on the cheek.

"You don't know what that can do for them," Reed said.

• • •

Jim Irwin had to go to the moon to find God.

Irwin, the eighth man to walk on the moon, said he had a much different experience than a Russian cosmonaut in the 1960s returning from space and telling the world that there isn't a God because he didn't see Him.

"It was just the opposite, not that I expected to see God, but I saw the handiwork, the precision and the plan...deeply sensing the plan that God has for outer space," Irwin said.

Irwin said that before the flight in 1971 he "never did anything to express my faith...I never was that religious. Now, I'm trying to make up for lost time.

"To see the beauty and uniqueness of the earth I was deeply aware that God had made a unique place for man to live."

Jim Irwin on moon

Irwin said he believed most of the men who went to the moon would admit "they felt closer to God on that flight."

Irwin heads High Flight, an evangelistic program to tell the world about the teachings of Jesus Christ. He is the author of *To Rule the Night*, his life's story and experiences of going to the moon.

• • •

Jim Dingman, a pastor of a small church outside Phoenix, visited migrant camps telling the workers and their children about the Lord. He and his wife, Vera, saw the need a home for needy children.

In 1954, the couple drove to the desert and saw a former boys' school on 155 acres. The buildings had been deserted for 20 years and there were holes in the floors and walls. "It looked just like an old dump," Vera said.

They sold their house, moved on the property and began fixing the place up with help from friends. When they finished, the state gave them a license to house 10 children. In a few days, 10 children moved into the new Sunshine Acres Children's Home.

For 12 years, Vera washed 30 loads of clothes daily in wringer-type washing machines.

More buildings were built and the home grew to house as many as 60 children. Donations came from people believing in the Dingman's work to raise neglected and problem children, allowing them to get a fresh start to face adulthood. The love shown to the children by the Dingmans, house parents and staff has produced success story after success story since the home was opened more than 50 years ago.

Once, police picked up an 8-year-old boy for stealing and brought him to Sunshine Acres. His mother was an alcoholic; he had no father.

"When he first came to us," recalled Vera, "he used mostly four-letter words, but in the Christian atmosphere of the home, he trusted Christ as Savior within a year." He graduated from high school earning athletic letters in football and wrestling. He also won a scholarship to a junior college.

After high school graduation, he spoke to the members of his church: "If I hadn't been sent to Sunshine Acres, I know I'd have spent my growing-up years in a reform school."

Note: Jim and Vera Dingman have since died, and family members are currently operating the school.

Jim and Vera Dingman (cicra 1980s)

You Sold Out, Eddy

As a pre-adolescent, I thought Eddy Arnold was one of the coolest singers alive. I loved his guitar-picking and especially his rendition of *Cattle Call*, with a smattering of yodeling that obviously reached the height of anyone's talent, I thought.

Entering adulthood, I lost track of idol Eddy. Then, in my 40s, my newspaper boss told me to review Arnold's upcoming concert in Sun City West. YaaaHoo! Pleasant memories of bygone years! I'll finally see my boyhood idol!

What a disappointment. At age 67 (this was in 1986), his voice leaned on the frail side compared to his strong, melodic sounds some 20 to 35 years before when he recorded such country and crossover hits as *Anytime, Make the World Go Away, Bouquet of Roses, That's How Much I Love You* and *What's He Doing in My World?*

When Arnold reached his peak in the 1950s, he appeared to have a clean-cut image. That image, though, appeared tainted when (at the Sun City West concert) he told an off-color joke about a man spending a night with a married woman and later being confronted by her husband. Another joke about a woman going to a masquerade party dressed as a cow and being met by a bull in a pasture also lowered my image of him. These jokes, as mild as some may view them now, did not seem to fit the style of the man known as the Tennessee Plowboy. It seemed Arnold did this to make up for a failing voice, and maybe to discount his clean image. How sad.

Arnold died May 8, 2008. In his Associated Press obituary, the reporter said the singer's image was always that of a modest, clean-cut country boy.

"You cannot satisfy all the people," Arnold once said. "They have an image of me. Some people think I'm Billy Graham's half brother, but I'm not. I want people to get this hero thing off their mind and just let me be me." I guess Arnold must have read my 1986 review on his concert.

I interviewed and covered concerts by many once-famous men singers in the 1980s. They, along with Eddy Arnold, were all past their prime if they admitted it or not. Many, but not all, should have given up years before and sailed into the sunset counting the money they earned when they had hit the top charts. They just didn't know when to fold 'em and quit, reminding me of Michael Jordan, the greatest basketball star ever, who came from retirement to return to the NBA. He hardly could make the first team. How sad, indeed.

Tom Jones, a heart-throb in the 1960s, insisted the pace of his show would be the same as in past years, but he admitted in an interview he was slowing down and spending more time at his California home. "I don't do it (months on the road at a time) straight through anymore," said Jones, 46 and a grandfather. His grown son, Mark, travels with him on tour and helps manage his father's show career.

Surprisingly, at his Sun City West concert in the 1980s, young women still flocked in front of the stage. For decades, his female fans threw not only flowers at him but also hotel keys and undergarments. However, at age 46, the gifts diminished with his age.

Engelbert Humperdinck, however, was different. His performance sparkled with vitality. He also was versatile. On one song, he yodeled (remember, I believe that's the height of singing talent), and on a couple of others he danced with lovely female dancers. He told jokes (a couple of them mildly shady), and called a married woman to come up on stage and he sang her a love song while her husband sat watching in the front row.

He never recorded anything greater than his decades-old hits – *Release Me, The Last Waltz, A Man Without Love, Am I That Easy to Forget, There Goes My Everything* and *Blue Spanish Eyes.* He received a standing ovation (the Sun City West Sundome's crowd gives almost everyone a standing ovation regardless how good or bad they were) and at the end a small army of women followers crowded the stage. Their arms reached out as Humperdinck threw about 10 monogrammed neckerchiefs at them.

Jim Nabors had a few hits, but he was most noted as the bumbling gasoline-station attendant, Gomer Pyle, on Andy Griffith's television show. He also had his own long-running show, *Gomer Pyle USMC*, and briefly hosted *The Jim Nabors Hour.*

He retired and bought 500 acres of Hawaiian jungle. He cleared the land and planted macadamia nut seedlings. The trees grew and produced nuts, making Nabors money. But, Nabors grew bored of resting on beaches counting money and watching his trees grow. He came out of retirement focusing on television again. He mainly struck out. His once sizzling TV career had fizzled.

"I did a (situation comedy) pilot this year (1986) for NBC, and it scored really well when they put it on the air," Nabors said. "They didn't give it any promotion or any advertisement whatsoever. They just stuck it on, and it still was a fraction of a point out of the top 10. Yet, they didn't buy it."

Singer Bobby Vinton, 49, the teen idol of the 1960s, convinced himself his music would rebound.

"My music is really coming back," he said during a '80s telephone interview. "I'm going back to what I did 20 years ago…I'm looking at my wall now as I talk to you, and I got about 60 albums on the wall and they sound like country music sounds today.

"When I listen to all the current country artists, what they call country today is what...my music was 20 years ago.

"So, going to Nashville with my style of music is nothing new for me. It's just that it is new for the country people 'cause they didn't realize that I was country before they were."

He recorded *Roses Are Red* decades ago. Before it became popular, he tried to get disc jockeys to play it. He bought an armload of roses, got a stack of his singles and visited local radio stations. (Note: This was in the ancient era when music was recorded on "records" and "albums," way before the creation of CDs, DVDs, the Ipod, etc.)

"I felt awkward...handing flowers to one of the guys. There was a pretty girl walking down the street with nice legs...I stopped her and said, 'See all these flowers I have here, I can't throw them away...would you do me a favor and take these flowers in to that disc jockey there?'"

She agreed. The disc jockey took the roses and record and played the song.

Vinton coaxed her to accompany him to other stations and hand out more flowers and records. He then gave her some flowers, and she walked away before he could learn her name. He never saw her again.

The radio stations began playing *Roses Are Red*, and soon the song became a national hit. After that, he had hit after hit. As with most high profile male singers in the '50s and '60s his star faded.

Vinton recorded a new song in the '80s called *Bed of Roses*. "If you see a girl with nice legs bringing a record...you'll know it's me up to my old tricks," he said, chuckling. Unfortunately for Vinton, *Bed of Roses* never rose in the charts as his earlier hits had done.

Singer Robert Goulet also was famous once. But decades after his heyday his frustration showed when he talked about records.

"Nobody else is going to hire me to record when the other baritones are wearing one glove and mascara. I have to do this on my own."

He was referring to Rove, the record company he formed in 1986 to release his album *Won't You Dance With This Man.*

"Many artists are doing the same thing today – Steve (Lawrence) and Eydie (Gorme) to Vic Damone, Howard Keel and Engelbert Humperdinck. They are not selling in record stores because, as you probably know, 70 percent of records are bought by teenagers – and I'm not sure how many teenagers know who the hell I am."

For those who don't know, Goulet's name skyrocketed across America in 1960 when, as a new kid on the block, he starred on Broadway in *Camelot.*

Through the years, he performed in movies and Las Vegas, on television specials and he had his own TV series. He won one Grammy and two Tony awards, and recorded more than 40 albums. But, that was a long time ago and Goulet seethes he's not on top anymore.

Sammy Davis Jr. was an exception to the has-been norm. Four months before his Sun City West Sundome gig, Davis had hip surgery and while recovering wondered if he would ever perform on stage again. "The man upstairs smiled at me," Davis said. He slipped on shiny tap shoes and executed machine-gun clicking of toes and heels as the 30-piece orchestra played *Tea for Two.* The 5,000 crowd went wild.

Davis entertained on stage without intermission for 105 minutes. His opening act didn't show up, and Davis stretched his performance to take up the slack. "I'm taking advantage of your presence," Davis said. "This kind of evening is better for me than medicine."

He sang a dozen standards and the only heavy metal during the show, he said, would be the six rings he wore on his fingers. Like a river carrying a leaf, the music playfully twisted, turned, ran swiftly and then gently but always enhanced Davis' singing.

Perry Como was 72 when he hit the Sundome stage. During his half-century in show business up to 1984, he had sold 100 million records. Although Como preferred to stay home on the inland waterway in Jupiter, Fla., his business associates convinced him to go on the concert trail for a couple months in 1984 to observe his 50 years in show business.

He admitted he thought some of the songs he recorded and became hits were pretty dumb.

"There are many songs that were brought up that I didn't particularly care for," Como said. "But anyone who was there who I had respect for, and listened to, would say, 'I think you ought to do it,' and we'd do it and we'd wind up with a gold record. You felt kind of stupid after a bit."

Two hits he thought were "dumb" were *Don't Let the Stars Get in Your Eyes*, on which he relented only long enough to do one take, and *Hot Diggity*.

"We complain about some of the stuff that the kids have today, but we had some pretty dumb stuff then," Como said. "Today, the lyric doesn't mean a hell of a lot."

Dixieland jazz clarinetist Pete Fountain carried his lunch box to work. Unlike others who perform before Sun City West audiences, Fountain probably didn't utter 150 words during his 90-minute concert. He and his 7-member band played almost continuously, and each song lasted about 10 minutes. He didn't believe shortchanging an audience with banter.

The 55-year-old entertainer had slowed down. He owned a club in New Orleans and when he wasn't there he could be found fishing from the pier at his home in Bay St. Louis or taking a boat into "what they call the Louisiana Marsh," he said.

"I've got to watch myself lately. I've been falling asleep with the pole in my hand. That's when you know you're getting old."

Fountain was one "has-been" who got his priority in order. He goes fishing a lot more times than going to work.

Note: Sammy Davis Jr. died in 1990, Perry Como died in 2001 and Robert Goulet died in 2007.

Female Has-Beens

A parade of female has-beens marched through Sun City West retirement community northeast of Phoenix during the 1980s. Ever heard of Peggy Lee, Connie Francis or Mitzi Gaynor?

These, and others, headlined marques some 25 years earlier. Their fame since had diminished. Never fear, though. They still trudged along the entertainment circuit appearing in front of much smaller crowds. The gray-hairs and bald heads in retirement communities still came out in droves, re-living when they were swinging blondes, redheads and brunets (and the men still had hair) and the has-been entertainers were on top of their game.

The old men in the audience especially enjoyed the shapely, and somewhat talented Suzanne Somers who still had the curves of a female 20 years younger. Suzanne exploited her body to the hilt with cleavage-revealing costumes that had hip-high slits.

Suzanne, Mitzi Gaynor, Charo and Debbie Reynolds strutted and pranced across the stage in skimpy outfits, believing talent and beauty mix. Their shows, they contend, will be enjoyed more if they expose both to the audience.

And the old fogies in the audience got a hoot when one of these entertainers went into the audience to rub the bald head of an elderly man, sit on his lap (this was before lap-dancing became the rage) or drag him onstage, cuddle real close and sang him a love song.

Afterward, as Suzanne did, the entertainer took the man back to his wife and told her, "See, I got him all warmed up for you."

Debbie Relynolds was in her 50s when she appeared in Sun City West. In her prime as an actress and singer, people regarded her as "the girl next door." But no more. Her act was purely nightclubish, sprinkled with risqué jokes and slams against actress Elizabeth Taylor, another has-been.

Twenty-five years earlier, Reynolds' first husband, Eddie Fisher, left home to marry Taylor. Later, Reynolds admitted in a magazine article she had encouraged Fisher to "go over and console Liz" after Taylor's husband, Mike Todd, had died in a plane crash in 1958.

"The whole world blamed Elizabeth (for Fisher's defection) but I didn't," Reynolds said of the breakup. "A man doesn't want to leave unless he wants to leave."

Realizing many in the audience still felt sorry for her, she slammed Taylor to get cheap laughs.

Reynolds said she refused to eat strawberry shortcake earlier in the day because "I just don't want to wind up looking like Elizabeth." Also, Reynolds said Taylor's legs looked like "condos." Then Reynolds sunk the barb deeper by showing off her own shapely legs to the audience.

Charo, a sexy, fun-loving song-and-dance woman, exuded a "kick-off-the-shoes-and-have-fun" attitude. She announced to the audience in a heavily accented voice: "Tonight, we are goin' to have a helluva good time."

And her energy and talent backed up that statement. Besides singing and dancing, she brought out her guitar and expertly played a medley of classical and flamenco numbers, including *Malaguena, Granada* and *Romance of Love*.

In an interview prior to the show, Charo very slowly in Spanish-accented English admitted: "I have a beeg problem. Eez my accent."

She said in personal appearances the accent was very charming to people, but when she tried to break into a serious role such as in movies or on Broadway the accent was a handicap. "Et's givin' me lotsa trouble."

She gets plenty of scripts, but her role always portrays the same type of character – a girl who comes from a Latin country who does "coochy-coochy."

"Et's taken me to nowhere," she said. "I want to (have more serious parts)...I dream about et, I want et to happen, but I don't know et is goin' to happen."

Charo was born Maria Rosario Pilar Martinez Molina Baeza in Murcia, Spain. At age 4, her parents sent her to a convent school where the nuns noticed her musical ability. At 15, she studied with some of Spain's leading classical guitarists, including Andres Segovia. Xavier Cugart discovered her, married her and brought her to the United States and Charo's fame began to rise on her own.

Not to be out-done, Mitzi Gaynor also has a long moniker – Francesca Mitzi Marlene de Charney von Gerber. She was born in Chicago in 1930.

Gaynor appeared on the Sun City West stage with an 18-piece orchestra and eight talented "musical men" who performed on their own along with dancing and singing with her. Gaynor traveled across the nation with her musicians and male dancers. Unlike some other entertainers, she puts together a new show of songs, dances and about a dozen costume changes each season. "I think that once you have paid your money...you shouldn't have to pay money again to see the same thing," she said. "It's only fair to my audience to bring them something new. Also, I get bored with the thing after a while."

Gaynor had hired two men to research the music for her shows.

"Some reviewers are so funny: everyone is trying to catch you on something," she said. "One time I was doing a set of songs (from) the '30s, and one song was written...like in December, 1929. (A reviewer wrote): 'Well, if Miss Gaynor would research this more…'

…I generally work with 10 dancers but sometimes somebody gets hurt, or somebody can't work or leaves, or I have
to let him go. I'll read, 'Miss Gaynor told me in an interview
that she has 10 dancers, and last night she only had nine.' I
can't stop the whole show and say that George sprained his
ankle in Chicago."

Peggy Lee, otherwise, sings alone on stage and is only
backed up by a quintet of musicians. Born in 1920, she started
singing with the Benny Goodman Band and then went off
on her own to record smash hits such as *Why Don't You Do
Right?*, *Fever*, *It's a Good Day*, *Big Spender*, *Lover*, *Manana* and *Is
That All There Is?* She had remained faithful to popular songs
and love ballads, recording some 60 albums and more than
600 songs. How did she survive when most of the country
turned to rock?

"There was one period that was momentarily my case
of future shock," she said. "That's when acid rock came in.
Hard rock! And, I really was almost knocked off my pins,
mentally speaking."

She's convinced there is still a groundswell of people
who like a gentler kind of music: "Wherever I've been playing, it's as though people are saying, 'Hello,' and more than
they ever did."

Connie Francis also rocketed as a singing idol in the late
'50s and early '60s. At one time, her record sales exceeded
80 million worldwide. Only Elvis Presley and the Beatles
sold more back then. In 1985, at age 46, Francis forged on the
comeback trail after a series of personal tragedies.

"I have my life together and am a very happy girl these
days," she said in a 1985 telephone interview. "Everything is
going right, and it is a nice feeling for a change."

Her decade of horror, shock and depression began when
an intruder raped and robbed her in a motel room in 1974.
In the following years, she lost her singing voice for four
years, her husband left her, her younger brother was slain
gangland-style in New Jersey, and her father committed her

to psychiatric hospitals for two brief periods in 1983. The following year, she took an overdose of sleeping pills and went to bed. In the morning, her housekeeper found her, still alive, and called an emergency unit. After recovering, Francis checked into a clinic.

She said she emerged as a more confident person bent on coping and making a living again.

"It is inconceivable to me that I could have been as depressed as I was then to know that I am sitting on top of the world these days," Francis said. "Every time you come through a bad experience you become stronger because you have more faith and confidence in yourself so you can weather those things."

Francis was born Concetta Rosa Maria Franconero on December 12, 1938. At age 16, she signed a contract with MGM Records, but her first 10 records failed. Dick Clark played one of her songs, *Who's Sorry Now?*, on his *American Bandstand* show and her break into stardom soared. The record sold a million copies in just two months.

Francis recorded hit after hit, including *Where The Boys Are, Lipstick on Your Collar* and *Everybody's Somebody's Fool.* She earned America's top female vocalist title by the music industry seven years in a row.

Francis has recorded her records in six languages – English, Spanish, Italian, German, Japanese and French. She speaks Spanish and Italian, and hires a teacher to help her learn the lyrics in Japanese, French and German.

And that extra work has paid off. "When I was at the peak of my recording career, 70 percent of all the revenue I earned came from foreign countries," she said.

• • •

And for all these female has-beens, royalties from their songs still trickle in and some still perform before live audiences. Memories of their star-lighted past keep them going. Note: Peggy Lee died in 2002.

Part Three – Places

Come with me to some interesting places including a cool spot in Norway to the pleasantly warm Sea of Galilee in Israel. Along the way we will stop at such places as a beach town in southern Portugal, Sitka (Alaska), Loretto (Mexico) and several other places in between. There's a soda water town in Colorado and a land of blue-green water people in the bottom of the Grand Canyon. Enjoy!

Dogology

ALBUFEIRA, Portugal – This little fishing village in the late 1960s had a run on dogs. So much in fact that Europeans – but surprisingly few Americans – have been coming here in increasing numbers to chase the dogs off the beaches and streets so they can enjoy the dog's life, too.

The dogs mirror the way of life in this village; from the shaggy mongrels in the poor fishermen quarter and stately hounds owned by retired Englishmen, to the playful beach whelps that romp on sand and surf and the lazy restaurant canines that curl in corners where tasty Portuguese cuisines are served.

"Dogology" is a favorite pastime, and conversations often turn to "those unusual dogs in Albufeira" among tourists sitting at the numerous sidewalk cafes.

"The king of the town," a brown and white dog, spends his days sitting on a purple pillow in Sir Harry's Bar; "the fisherman," a black mongrel, rides in the small fishing craft on the tossing sea; "the town's beggar," a bulldog that always has bloodshot eyes, stares at tourists in restaurants until he is tossed a bone, and "the town's cop," a small pooch that sits and guards the same alley day after day.

"Dogology" is only an added attraction in Albufeira

where spring comes in late January when the countryside bursts with white and pink almond blossoms. Also in January, it is possible to lie on the beach and get a tan.

Albufeira is in the middle of Portugal's Algarve section; 100 miles of beaches and cliffs on the country's southern border. Among Europeans, it is starting to be called the "Portuguese Riviera."

The Algarve coastline is protected from the cold winds from the north by a mountain range. Temperatures average in the 70s in the summer and 50s in the winter.

Although first class and luxury hotels are springing up all along the coast anticipating a tremendous tourist boom (which has happened of late), little has affected the lives of the Algarvians who still depend heavily on wrestling fish away from the Atlantic Ocean for a livelihood.

The tourists' cost-of-living in Albufeira is among the lowest anywhere in Europe. In Pensao Albufeirense, a modern boardinghouse that has hot and cold running water in all rooms, a single with Continental breakfast starts at $1.40 a night and double at $2.10. A room including all meals is $3.50 and $6.30 respectively. Winter rates are even lower. (Note: today's rate in 2008 is about $40 a night, still a great bargain. Other prices in this article are based on 1968 rates.)

For those on a starvation budget, rooms in private homes are less expensive than in boardinghouses. There is a "Turismo" office near the beach that helps tourists find rooms.

Albufeira, population 15,000 including families living in the nearby countryside, is built on two hills. Its whitewash houses with red and brown tile roofs sweep down these hills to meet the blue sea and open sky.

The beach at Albufeira, shaped like a boomerang, is considered the warmest of all beaches in the Algarve because cliffs lining it radiate the sun's rays to bathers. It is a favorite place for winter vacationers. A tunnel through a hill leads from the town to the beach.

A movie theater, built is 1947, shows American and English movies with Portuguese subtitles four nights a weeks.

Several native restaurants are in Albufeira where in 1968 for $1, a person can get soup, salad, rolls, a meat or fish dish, potatoes, a small pitcher of wine, a small plate of olives and dessert, which usually includes an orange, apple or banana.

Favorites with foreigners are "caldo verde" soup made with mashed potatoes and finely shredded kale; "bacalhau," a cod fish; and "cozido a Portuguesa," a mixture of beef and pork boiled with cabbage, potatoes, rice, vegetables, bacon and various sausages.

Early every morning, local farmers haul fruits and vegetables in horse- and mule-driven carts to the open-air marketplace in the center of town. Several Sundays during the year a "market fair" is held and vendors throughout the Algarve bring their goods to Albufeira. The marketplace overflows into side streets and pigs, trees, canned squid, grain, shoes, chairs, pottery, copperware and chickens are sold. Portuguese arrive by bus loads.

However, for the locals, the big event in town is every Saturday night when the town's only mannequin, a shapely blond with two missing fingers, gets decked out in a new sexy dress or nightgown. The Portuguese gather in front of the store – which caters to tourists and the English colony living here – and gaze and make comments; the men in low wolf whistles and the long-skirted women with laughter.

The heart of the community, however, is the fishermen quarter. Scores of Phoenician-type boats painted in bright blues, reds, yellows, greens, black and white line the beach.

Many of the boats have Portuguese inscriptions such as "Guide us God into the High Seas," and "God Lights the Good Way." Some of the words are misspelled.

The fishermen usually take these boats out in early evening and drop mile-long nets and baited lines into the ocean. They stay out all night; the gas lanterns on their small craft look like fireflies on the dark ocean.

In the morning, the boats come in and the fish are sold to

merchants in the nearby fish market for the highest bid. The fishermen spend much of the day untangling and repairing nets and lines.

The older men, who are past their prime to go out in boats, earn money by pulling in the huge net from shore. When the fish are running, nine men row a large boat into the Atlantic dropping a cable as they go. One end is tied to a stake on shore and the other to the net. When the end of the cable is reached a half-mile out, the net is dropped and the men row back, letting out another cable tied to the other end of the net.

On shore, the old men form two lines some 30 yards apart and pull the cables in, a process that takes two hours. Just before the net reaches shore, one of the men walks into the sea and "spanks" the water with a broken oar. They believe this prevents a last minute escape by the fish.

Some days the labors of the 25 to 30 men earn a catch of $30, other days only $6 or $7.

Scattered throughout the fishermen quarter are a number of wine shops where a glass of wine costs less than two cents. When work is finished, the fishermen in their knee-high boots and patched trousers and shirts drift into these shops and sit and talk the night away.

One shop has a television set and the men sit almost spellbound watching such programs as *Dr. Kildare* and *Disneyland*.

Albufeira is 200 miles south of Lisbon. The five-hour train ride in 1968 costs $3. An airplane flight to Faro, Algarve's largest and most cosmopolitan city, costs $11. The 25-mile train trip from Faro will set a person back another 35 cents.

From Albufeira many side trips can be taken inexpensively. Trains and buses fan out to practically all villages and beaches in the Algarve. The cost to the farthest point is less than $1.25.

Thirty-five miles northwest of Albufeira is the tiny settlement of Caldes de Monchique, nestled in a lonely valley and shadowed by heavy woods. Nearby is an ancient Roman spa with waters still reputed to cure skin diseases and rheumatism.

Two miles up the mountain is "Paraiso dal Montanha," a native restaurant with a reputation spreading throughout the Algarve. The specialty is a delicious fried chicken basted with a hint of hot pepper sauce. A small fryer and soup, bread, potatoes and customary wine cost $1.40.

At the top of the mountain is Foia, which gives visitors the best view of the Algarve. Farm land and woods stretch below like a patched carpet all the way to the sea.

Throughout the Algarve are numerous grottoes, forts and old churches and monasteries to explore. Albufeira is the best stepping-off point to the Algarve.

Along with its dogs, Albufeira is unusual in other ways, too. The town's five taxis are Mercedes Benzes; a bottle of wine can be bought for 26 cents but a can of tomato soup costs 31 cents, and it's legal to double park on its streets. Both dog and man can have their day here.

Ship Ahoy, Tourist

INLAND PASSAGE, Alaska -- Alaskans like to snub their noses at Texans. At 586,412 square miles, you can cut Alaska in half and make two states. Texas would still be only the third largest state in the nation.

And more people are finding Alaska on the map. People in the lower 48 states annually flock to this 49th state in increasing numbers. A favorite way to see part of this intriguing land that harbors whales, totem poles and bald eagles is to take a cruise between May and September.

In 2006, a total of 27 large cruise ships plus numerous ferries hauled an estimated million passengers to the state, which one promotional Alaskan DVD claims has 3 million lakes (a snub to Minnesota that only has 10,000 lakes) and 100,000 glaciers. Juneau, the only land-locked state capital in the U.S. (the 40-mile highway through town dead ends against rugged mountains at both ends), swells in the summer hosting about 600,000 cruise-ship passengers.

"There are only three ways to get to Juneau...ship, air and birth canal," said Case Swderus, a Gray Line bus tour guide in Juneau. He was busy hauling passengers around Juneau one summer day after Holland America's Westerdam cruise ship landed in port for a few hours. In 2008, eight Holland

America ships cruised Alaska's shores.

Swderus was full of tidbits about Juneau while driving us to stops at Macaulay Salmon Hatchery and Mendenhall Glacier.

In 1930, officials in the new municipal building furnished the third floor with the town's post office. It later was discovered that some obscure federal law mandated that post offices couldn't be any higher than the second floor.

The Juneau government bosses didn't want to haul the post office's heavy equipment down a flight of stairs so they came up with this clever solution, Swderus said. The first floor became the "ground floor," and the second floor became the "first floor" and thus, the post office was officially on the second floor without moving an inch.

Swderus drove by a statue of several pelicans in front of a municipal building. There are no pelicans in Alaska. The tour guide explained that a city in Florida commissioned a sculptor to make a pelican sculpture about the same time officials in Juneau commissioned the same sculptor to make a statue of bald eagles. The sculptor mixed up the orders and sent the bald eagles to Florida, and the pelicans to Juneau. The Florida town refused to send the bald eagles back because they liked it better and Juneau was stuck with the pelicans.

(Another oddity: Lew Brantley, the naturalist on ship, said an Alaskan fisherman caught a weird-looking fish in his net and he didn't know what it was. The fisherman took the fish to a biologist who identified it as a tuna. Tuna, like pelicans, prefer a warmer climate and don't reside in Alaska. The tuna was stuffed. Alaskans still chuckle at the pelican and tuna displays.)

Cruise lines do more than just sail to Alaskan towns, glaciers, inlets, passages and fjords. On special cruises, you can get off and for a few days and fly or take a motor coach or train to such places as the Yukon, Anchorage, Denali National Park, Prudhoe Bay in the Arctic Circle, Fairbanks and the foothills of towering 20,320-foot Mt. McKinley.

The seven-day Westerdam (embark and debark in Seattle)

cruised over 1,300 miles the first two days to reach Hubbard Glacier, which Frommer's *Alaska Cruises & Ports of Call* contends is more impressive to see than the more traveled and popular Glacier Bay National Park to the south along the state's inside passage.

After entering Yakutat Bay, the ship sailed up to the six-mile wide glacier that was much taller than the 11-storied ship. It was a somewhat sunny day when the Westerdam arrived and for an hour the passengers ooohed and aaawed as parts of the glacier "calved," sending huge chunks of bluish-tinted ice into the sea causing large sprays of water and waves.

One small iceberg floated near the ship and the part under water must of hit the ship. The iceberg, which throughout is under tremendous pressure, burst and fizzled like a giant Alka-Seltzer with chunks of ice crumbling in all directions. The once iceberg was now in hundreds of smaller pieces.

After touring Hubbard Glacier, the 1,848-passenger Westerdam sailed the next few days in the Alaskan Inside Passage allowing guests to get off and explore Juneau, Sitka, Ketchikan and Victoria, British Columbia, Canada.

At each stop there were a slew of shore excursions (for an extra fee) for passengers to take. Some of these include historical town tours, dog sledding on a glacier via a helicopter ride, kayaking, gold mine tour, salmon fishing and bake, snorkeling, floatplane tour, whales and bear watching, Harley-Davidson motorcycle tour and Victoria ale and pub tour.

Some highlights at each town:

Juneau – Highly recommended is the historical bus tour through town with stops at Macaulay Salmon Hatchery and, 13 miles away, Mendenhall Glacier and visitor center.

A tour guide at the hatchery explains that salmon return to their place of birth at the hatchery after living in the Pacific Ocean. Eggs from the females are collected and fertilized with the sperm from the males. The fry will spend 9 to 12 weeks at the hatchery before they are released to spend 2 to 5 years in the ocean before returning to the hatchery to complete the salmon life-cycle.

Mendenhall Glacier is not as impressive as Hubbard Glacier, but the surrounding area is full of short hiking trails and creeks where salmon flourish and a bear may wander in from time to time. The visitor center is chock full of interpretive programs and exhibits, kids programs, a glacier observatory and a bookstore.

Mount Roberts Tramway rises 1,800 feet to spectacular views of the town and surrounding forest. Included are a hiking trail, nature center, the showing of a film about the native Tlingit Indians, gift shop and restaurant.

A must is Juneau's landmark Red Dog Saloon that serves tasty food in a frontier atmosphere. A honky-tonk piano player spews one-liners. A sign tells customers: "If our food, drinks and service aren't up to your standards, please lower your standards!"

Also, you can buy Red Dog panties for $8: "Ever find yourself on a luxury cruise-liner in Alaska with no clean underwear? We've got you covered with our bright red nylon and lace ladies panties."

Sitka – A flight of stairs lead to the top of Castle Hill, which overlooks the town, harbor and surrounding mountainous terrain. It is here on Oct. 18, 1867 that Russia sold its holdings of Alaska to the United States for $7.2 million in gold, or less than 2 cents an acre. The Russian flag was lowered and the U.S. flag was raised for the first time on Alaskan soil. Sitka was Alaska's first capital before the honor was moved to Juneau in 1912.

Sitka, with about 9,000 year-round population 95 miles southwest of Juneau, still maintain its Russian heritage. St. Michael's Russian Orthodox Cathedral with onion-shaped dome highlights the downtown district. Valuable paintings and icons, most brought over on ship in 1813, are displayed. The original church caught fire in 1966, but before the fire could spread 100 people formed human chains to haul out the contents. They saved 95 percent of the artwork and furnishings including a 300-pound chandelier. The cathedral, rebuilt in 1976, is a replica of the original.

The all-female Russian New Archangel folk dancers perform when cruise-ship passengers are in town. The troupe was organized in 1969 and the men in town refused to participate because they didn't think Russian folk dance performances would ever draw a crowd. They were wrong, and tourists flocked to see the dances. The men asked to be part of the troupe, but the women refused. The women, sometimes wearing false beards when appropriate, wear both male and female costumes and perform both gender roles during routines.

Sitka National Historical Park, the site where the Russians and the Tlingits Indians fought a fierce battle in 1804, features a totem pole walking trail; Isabel Miller Museum features the town's history with photographs, documents and artifacts including a diorama of Sitka as it was in 1867; Alaska Raptor Rehabilitation Center houses injured raptors including bald eagles (if restored to health they will be released in the wild), and Whale Park provides viewing of wildlife including humpback whales in fall and early spring.

Ketchikan – The mountain range hugs close to shore and Ketchikan's founders were left with little space to expand the town. These enterprising pioneers added "land" by sinking sturdy pilings and building piers. Today, some of the buildings are on stilts in the harbor. Even along the infamous Creek Street (a former red-light district until prostitution was outlawed in 1953), the wooden buildings are on stilts overlooking Ketchikan Creek. These buildings have been converted into jewelry, t-shirt and other tourist shops.

It is along Ketchikan Creek salmon swim upstream to spawn in the gravel beds. The fish even leap on the man-made, concrete salmon-ladder to reach higher spawning waters.

The Southeast Alaska Discovery Center houses a museum about the town's history when it once was portrayed as the "Salmon Capital of the World." Saxman Native Village Totem Pole Park features the revival of Native arts and culture with sculptors chiseling out new totem poles.

There are two walking tours that feature various totem poles, cannery cottages and other historical buildings, Creek Street including Dolly House (a brothel left virtually untouched), Tongass Historical Museum (depicting the town's venture as a native fish camp, mining hub, salmon-canning capital, fishing port and timber town), and hatchery and eagle center.

Ketchikan's buildings hanging over creek

Victoria – Sitka has the Russian flavor, but Victoria is strictly British amid its tea rooms, Victorian houses, double-deck buses and horse-drawn carriages. The Westerdam just docked here for a short time to allow cruisers to just get a glimpse of this fascinating city with its manicured flower gardens including Butchart Gardens, and artists and performers delighting crowds on the waterfront. It is hard not to gawk at the magnificent Fairmont Empress Hotel and nearby parliament building. Miniature World museum features scenes of a circus, the world of Dickens, an enchanted valley of castles and the U.S. Civil war.

While on board sailing between ports, and to while away time, there are numerous activities and amenities available to guests. The 11-storied ship offers an internet room with computer classes; a library; fitness center; culinary demonstration; Las Vegas-type shows featuring singers, dancers, an illusionist and juggler; a casino; naturalist talks; whale-watching; gift shops; swimming pools; spa and salon; Bingo with over $1,500 jackpot; talent contest; raffle for a free Caribbean cruise; art auction; daily Catholic Mass; golf putting and a dozen or so restaurants and bars to visit.

A favorite pastime is to stand at the railing and scan the sea with binoculars to see killer and humpback whales soaring out of the water and then crashing the surface exploding a huge spray of water. The whales submerge with only their T-shaped tails waving for a second in the air.

Brantley, the onboard naturalist, tells the story of two killer whales working in tandem to eat some sea lions. The lions were on a small iceberg and one whale went under one end of the iceberg tipping it. The lions slid into the water and into the mouth of the second whale.

Crew members served champagne twice during the trip – at Capt. Peter Harris' reception early in the trip and at an embarkation briefing and introduction of crew members the last full day on board.

Some cruise tourists aren't the brightest light on deck. Ask any cruise director on board for the dumbest questions people ask him. (1.) "Does the crew sleep on board each night?" (No, they are flown in and out by helicopter) (2.) "What is the elevation of the cruise?" (3.) "What side of the ship do you see the whales?" (4.) And, before embarking, a guy complained he asked for the ocean-side stateroom and all he saw was tall buildings.

Here are some more:

(5.) "What do you do with ice carvings after they melt?" (6.) "What religion are the people with patches behind their ears?" (7.) "The captain announced that there are humpback whales off port at 3 o'clock. A woman looked at her watch and said, "It's 4:30, why do they tell us now." (8.) "Do these stairs go up or down?" (9.) "Will the elevator take me to the front of the ship?" (10.) "Will I get wet on the snorkeling tour?" (11. "Where can I get the bus for the walking tour?" (12.) "Honey, is that island surrounded by water?" (13.) "Does the ship dock in the center of town?" (14.) "Can I go to the singles and solo party if I'm married?"

Cost for the cruise varies according to how far in advance you book, date of sail, type of stateroom (inside or outside with or without verandah or private balcony) and on what deck. A nice outside stateroom 254-square-foot with verandah and queen-size bed on the sixth deck booked at least six months in advance cost just over $3,800 for a couple. This includes seven nights on board, all meals and snacks and use of most facilities. Soda drinks and alcoholic beverages are extra. On-shore excursions and meals are at your own expense.

Since more cruise lines going to Alaska use Seattle to embark and disembark, it is suggested to spend an extra day or two there before or after the cruise. A must visit is Pike Place Market, a multi-storied farmer's market that goes down to the waterfront.

Eight farmers hauled their produce to the area on Aug. 17, 1907, and about 10,000 residents flocked to the market. This scant beginning has mushroomed where today hundreds of stalls and stores (and about 55 restaurants) pack the marketplace. Along with fish, meat, produce, pastry and flowers, there also are dozens of shops selling such things as Tibet trinkets and tattoos to miniature cars and maps.

A short walk from Pike Place to Pier 57 is The Crab Pot, a delightful place for lunch. Try the popcorn shrimp and calamari strips appetizers (each for $7.25), or the "seafeasts for two," ranging from $13.95 to $29.95 per person. A bucket of fresh seafood including crab, shrimp in the shell, steamed clams and mussels, corn on the cob, red potatoes, sausage and halibut and salmon on a skewer is poured on the table on butcher paper.

A mallet and bib are passed out. You can whack away at the shelled seafood to get any frustrations out.

And, the best part, the food is "to live for." Who would want to "die" for it? What a stupid expression! You never could taste this gourmet delight again!

Mendenhall Glacier

Red Dog Saloon with Westerdam ship

Sitka from sea

Russian New Archangel folk dancers

Havasu Falls

Blue-Green Water People

SUPAI, Arizona – As long as the white man has money, the Havasupais will be happy. Nestled in a side canyon on the bottom of Arizona's Grand Canyon is this tiny Indian farming village, the capital of the Havasupai nation. The tribe has about 650 members and all but 200 of them live in this idyllic setting amid a gurgling creek, shade trees and cool, turquoise ponds beneath waterfalls.

About 30,000 people a year visit Supai, equipped with a

24-unit lodge, a campground for 250 guests and a café serving breakfast, lunch and dinner. Supai has become a Shangri-la for city-weary Arizonans and out-of-state tourists who want to rough it visiting this tiny Indian reservation. There is no television or telephone in the rooms and porta-potties are scattered around the campground. One amenity, however, is that the rooms are air-conditioned.

The only way to reach Supai is to drive to Hilltop, the canyon's edge, and either hike or ride horses and mules 3,000 feet down a hairpin trail and through winding side canyons to the green fertile valley. A general store is there for canned goods, meats, fruits and vegetables and other camping necessities.

At one time, up until the latter part of the 1900s, people would come to this valley without reservations and without paying any fees. That has changed now. You must now make reservations in advance and pay a $35 entrance fee. Add $5 per person for an environment-care fee. That will be refunded if you haul out a sack of garbage to hilltop. If you want a roof over your head, add about $145 a room per night. Campground fee is $17 daily per person. If you want to ride a horse or mule, instead of hiking, add another $150 roundtrip.

Two telephone wires strung through the canyons and over the highland plateau to Peach Springs, 80 miles away, and Grand Canyon Village, 50 miles away, connect Supai with the outside world. During storms, the lines are sometimes knocked out of service for days. Mail is toted on mules twice a week to the village.

Before the tourist explosion that began in the 1960s, the Havasupais barely eked out an existence (aside from collecting money from tourists) from crops and raising off-reservation grazing cattle. Many were miserably poor and depended heavily on welfare and other assistance programs. Now, according to the tribe's webpage, "Our people do not receive any government stipends and we pay income taxes just like all Americans."

In 1963-64, tourism accounted for $34,000 or about half of the tribal income. In 1975, tourism receipts reached $200,000, and the amount has been climbing ever since. Many of the Indians make their living packing tourists in-and-out of the valley.

Supai valley originally covered 518 acres at the foot of towering red sandstone canyon walls. In 1975, Congress added 185,000 acres "of our original hunting grounds back to the tribe." Many different kinds of fruits and vegetables are grown there – peaches, figs, pears, corn, beans, apricots, apples and squash. Lately, some of the fertile land has been neglected because of the tourist trade.

Several springs about a mile from the village create Havasu Creek that flows through the valley 11 miles to the Colorado River. The creek tumbles over a series of spectacular waterfalls – Navajo, Havasu, Mooney and Beaver. Beneath the falls are turquoise-hue pools, which are sheer delight for photographers shooting pictures or weary hikers plunging in for refreshing dips.

The creek is heavily impregnated with mineral salts of calcium and magnesium carbonates, calcium sulfate and magnesium chloride, which give off the blue-green coloring.

Taking the name from the water, the Indians have become known as the blue-green people. (Havasu, blue or green water; pai, people) The Havasupai Indians are happy-go-lucky most of the time. There is no hurry because tomorrow is a better time to do things than today. If they have to see a neighbor across the dirt road, they usually go on a horse. They laugh at almost anything.

Many outsiders underestimate the intelligence of these Indians. One tourist asked a young brave if he had a clock?

"No," the man said, as he walked away disgustedly. Another tourist heard him mutter: "But, I've got a watch."

Often the Indians will gather for their favorite sport – gambling.

They usually assemble at the far ends of the canyon. Their

laughter, shouting and screaming can be heard a mile away. Their gambling is similar to the American shell game.

They bet horses, food, clothing and even trees. It is possible for a peach tree to be blooming 10 feet from a family's house, but they can't pick the fruit. It was gambled away and another family owns it that lives about two miles up the canyon.

Many years ago, the tribal council ordered a piano from a Phoenix firm. The store's motto: "We'll deliver pianos anywhere in the state."

Two of the firm's employees loaded the piano in a truck and got to the canyon edge without mishap. Then they packed the instrument on horses and started the grueling eight-mile trip to the Indian settlement.

After about an hour of struggling with the load, the horses gave out. The men gave up. They set the piano in the middle of the trail and headed home.

The next day, the store changed its motto. The Indians had to deliver their own piano to the village.

In the 1950s, before tourists and civilization made such a major impact on the lives of the Havasupais, the 21-year-old wife of the tribe's medicine man was taken outside the canyon to a hospital. She was eight months pregnant.

She didn't like it there. So, she left and hiked 50 miles under the June Arizona sun back to Supai.

After she arrived in the village, complications set in. The medicine man brought his wife to the village missionary. He turned the mission into a maternity ward and delivered a baby boy. A doctor arrived in a helicopter a few hours later and the woman again was taken to the hospital. Today, Supai has a clinic along with a church and police station.

There have been missionaries in this canyon for decades. The Episcopal church made national headline in 1948 when a Quonset hut chapel was brought into the canyon by two helicopters. The church operated the mission until 1956. It was then leased to the United Indian Missions, an interdenominational group.

However, it was in 1927 when Christianity first came to Supai. Florence Barker was sent to the canyon to give medical aid to the Indians. During her seven-year stay, she taught the Indians Christianity from the Bible.

For 25 years after she left, the Havasupais remembered her instruction. In 1956, the tribal council met and invited the Unit-

At village store (circa 1950s)

ed Indian Missions to send a missionary. They had one prerequisite. They asked David Clark, general director of the mission at that time, "Do you believe the same as Mrs. Barker did?"

Clark said, "Yes." He visited the canyon to see if a missionary venture could be started. As soon as he arrived, two Indian women asked to be baptized. As girls, they became Christians under Mrs. Barker's teachings.

Clark sent the Rev. and Mrs. David Chambers to Supai. The couple found that the Indians live in the "here and now" and it's hard for them to live by faith as the Bible teaches.

Many times Chambers was called on to carry sick babies out of the canyon on horseback and, at Hilltop, climb into a parked vehicle and drive them to the Grand Canyon Hospital.

A dark cloud hung over this peaceful valley in 2006. On May 9, a Japanese tourist was murdered, and tribal officials have since refused to talk to the media. They even have escorted Japanese reporters out of the canyon. The tribe even posted a sign banning reporters. The woman was stabbed

29 times and left in shallow water near Navajo Falls. A 19-year-old Indian man was arrested. In September, 2007, he pleaded guilty to second-degree murder and was sentenced to life in prison without possibility of release. Robbery was the motive.

Hilltop is 70 miles from I-40 near Peach Springs. You can park your car there. Look over the canyon's edge. As far as the eye can see, there is nothing but bare, sandy hills, eroded by time, jutting from the canyon floor. A white, threadlike trail is seen going around a couple of hills and then vanishes. Supai can't be seen, but it's there, with the thunder of the waterfalls, the green fields and the laughter of the Indians.

Soda Water Town

MANITOU SPRINGS, Colorado – On a sidewalk corner in this hillside community in the shadow of Pike's Peak is a mineral spring that continuously spews water from a pipe.

People line up to drink or fill water jugs. I waited patiently in line recently. A boy of about 12 or 13 stood in front of me and when it was his turn, he bent over and sucked in a mouthful of water.

"Phew," he gasped, spitting out the water. "This is sick."

I smiled, and filled an empty two-liter plastic cola bottle with the delicious soda water. I hurried back to my nearby rented cabin so I could share this liquid treasure with the rest of my tourist party. Not everyone, I learned, can stomach this strong mineral drink.

The mineral spring water, which is noted for its curative powers, made this town. People not only drink it, but also sit in it at the Manitou Health Spa. After a bath, a person can get a stress massage from a student therapist for a nominal charge.

Centuries ago, Indians came to the site with their sick. They considered this area sacred and that the medicinal waters were a gift from the Great Spirit "Manitou."

By the 1870s, after the arrival of white settlers, Manitou Springs had become a thriving spa resort, and health seekers from as far away as Europe sought its cure.

Today, the town – located a few miles west of downtown Colorado Springs – is a sleepy hamlet awakening and catering to a growing tourist industry. Some of the 1930s' games in the penny arcade in the center of town actually cost only a penny. Yet, the town is a stepping-off point to some of the most sought-after attractions in Colorado, such as Pike's Peak, Garden of the Gods, Royal Gorge Canyon and Bridge, Cave of the Winds, North Pole (Santa's Village), Seven Falls and the century-old Cripple Creek gold-mining town.

The shop owners in Manitou Springs and Cripple Creek, an hour's drive into the hills, have a sense of humor.

C.C. Antique Emporium's sign states: "Anyone caught shoplifting will be forced to listen to Nancy Sinatra records."

In another shop, a sign on a chair reads: "reserved for the husband whose wife is 'just looking.'"

At Mary West's candy store the posted hours on the door announces that Mary West is semi-retired and that the store will be open weekdays from "9 a.m. to tired."

Messages on t-shirts hawk the area: "Life's a Mountain, not a Beach," and "I CLIMBED PIKE'S PEAK." On closer examination on the latter T-shirt, small print "into a tour bus to see" is stuck between "CLIMBED" and "PIKE'S."

At least one full day should be spent exploring Manitou Springs on foot: visiting the shops selling wares ranging from Indian crafts to leather goods; sampling sweets at The Fudge Factory; sitting on a bench in front of a bakery nibbling a fresh-baked cinnamon roll; taking a mineral springs walking tour, or strolling through Miramont Castle, a 46-room museum featuring nine styles of architecture.

The Wheeler Town Clock highlights the center of town. Jerome Wheeler, a rich banker in the area, donated this clock in 1889 for the opening of the Manitou Mineral Water Bottling Company. The clock, cast in Italy, initially was a fountain.

Unusual shop in Manitou Springs

Water flowed from dolphin heads into bowls. The statue on top depicts the goddess Hygeia, daughter of Aesclepius, Greek god of health and medicine. The fountain-part has long since disappeared, but the goddess still stares at the throngs of gawkers below.

Popular attractions within a 50-mile radius include:

*Pike's Peak Cog Railway, which is billed as the world's highest cog railway, takes visitors on a trip to the 14,110-foot summit. The season is May through October. Reservations required. Admission charged. Or, for the adventurer, drive your car on the switchbacks to the top. A restaurant and gift shop awaits you.

*Garden of the Gods is a 1,350-acre park showcasing red sandstone rock formations that were unusually sculpted through eons of time by erosion. The trading post, constructed in the style of Pueblo Indian homes, was established in 1900. It sells Indian jewelry, arts, crafts and Colorado gift items.

*North Pole is a story-land village where Santa sits and talks to children from mid-May through Dec. 24. Attractions include rides, petting zoo, magic shows and ubiquitous gift shops. Also, North Pole, Colo., has its own post office. Admission charged.

*U.S. Air Force Academy is on 18,000 acres featuring the 17-spired, inter-denominational chapel, planetarium and the academy visitor center. The chapel is open daily for public viewing unless a special service is being held. Try to get to the academy at 12:10 p.m. on weekdays during the academic year. That is when about 4,400 cadets march to lunch.

*Cave of the Winds has offered tours since 1881 along its mile of passageways. See stalactites, stalagmites and other formations such as massive limestone canopies on a 40-minute tour. Colored lights enhance the beauty of this underground fantasy adventure. For hard-core spelunkers, take the "wild tour" with a guide for two hours exploring with your flashlight as you crawl, climb and slide through tunnels and rooms into the heart of the mountain. Reservations needed for this latter tour.

*Cripple Creek, a gold-mining camp that produced no less than 28 millionaires, hit its peak in 1901 when the mines in the area yielded $25 million in gold. Gold mining has stopped, but one mine – the Mollie Kathleen – has re-opened as a tourist attraction. Guides take visitors 1,000 feet underground for tours. All told, there were 500 mines in the area, leaving a maze of more than 1,000 miles of tunnels. Today, the year-round population is 700, as compared to 5,000 during the boom years. Other attractions include numerous shops, a ride on the Cripple Creek & Victor Narrow Gauge Railroad, and gold-panning for "specks" of real gold.

*Royal Gorge Bridge was spanned in 1929 and is the world's highest suspension bridge, 1,055-feet above the raging Arkansas River. There are other ways to examine the canyon than just standing on the bridge and looking down. Try the aerial tramway across the gorge, the incline railway to the bottom, or bob on the river in a raft. Also, there is a children's creative playground, craft village, multi-media theater, shops and restaurants.

*Seven Falls, just a half-hour drive from Manitou Springs,

is a series of seven separate falls that splash and tumble 300 feet down granite cliffs. From mid-May through mid-September the entire canyon is illuminated with colored lights, including the seven falls.

After a day of sight-seeing, an evening at the Flying W Ranch for a chuck-wagon supper and Western show is popular among tourists. On a busy night about 1,400 people are each fed slices of beef, baked potato, beans, chunky applesauce, biscuits, old-fashioned spice cake and coffee or lemonade. The dinners are served from mid-May through the end of September both rain and shine. There is both outdoor and indoor seating. The cowboys entertain after the dinner with music, storytelling and jokes.

Also, some of the best yodeling west of the Mississippi River reverberates from the Flying W stage.

Apple Pickers

ALPINE TOWNSHIP, Michigan – Each year, a man who once lived in this area north of Grand Rapids would look forward to Fall. That's apple-picking time in these parts. He had retired from the U.S. Post Office and this seasonal work supplemented his income.

Alpine Township is in the heart of apple country. This area is noted to have the largest concentration of grower-owned apple storage facilities in the world. There are about 180 storehouses with a total capacity of more than 2 million bushels.

The man hauled his ladder to the orchard and picked an over-abundant tree with apples weighing heavily on its limbs. He would lean the ladder against the trunk, climb the ladder and start picking apples, dropping them into his cloth bag. There is a method to pick apples. You just don't grab the fruit and yank it off the tree. You have to gently caress the apple, slightly turning it so it will come off its stem. If that doesn't work and the stem is still attached, gently twist the stem until it comes off. Apple farmers warn new hirelings to do it that way so not to bruise the fruit.

For this man's labor he is paid 50 cents a bushel. Maybe he'll pick 60 bushels for $30 a day.

Alpine Township is one of Michigan's 1,242 townships. These townships govern the majority of the state's land mass. The townships serve almost 50 per cent of Michigan's residents.

Alpine Township's population is nearly 14,000, and its area is 36 square miles. It is a rural/urban township with 60 percent of its population living in the southeast corner, where M-37 highway runs through it creating an extensive commercial corridor with an industrial path and tracts of houses and condos.

However, more than 75 per cent of the township is rural, producing such agricultural products as apples, vegetables, bedding plants, flowers and dairy and beef cattle.

The rolling land and enriched soil is ideal for apple orchards. At first, the farmers hauled their apples to markets and distributors in nearby Grand Rapids. But now the farmers capitalize by cutting the middleman and storing and selling their own apples for larger profits.

Henry Kraft gets credit for that, according to David Weir in his book, *150 Years of Alpine Township History,* published in 1997. Much of the material in this article comes from Weir's book.

In 1910, Kraft loaded bushels of apples on a wagon pulled by three horses and went to Grand Rapids. He received 95 cents a bushel. A few months later, Kraft learned his apples were sorted into two grades, and the buyer paid $3 a bushel for the better grade and $2 a bushel for the other grade.

He wondered how he could store his apples on his farm and sell them to buyers instead of hauling them 18 miles in a wagon and get just a fraction of what they were worth.

He faced the problem of keeping the fruit cool long enough to sell on the open market.

A tile salesman helped solve the problem. Build a storage shed using two walls of tile, separated by a two-inch air space between, he suggested. Insulation would be used between the walls.

Kraft would open the doors to the storage shed at night

to let in the cool air, and shut the doors air-tight during the day.

Neighbors copied the idea and built their own storage facilities. When rural electricity came to Alpine Township in the 1930s, the farmers could use coolers to keep the fruit at 32 degrees.

The apple business in Alpine thrived, but in the summer of 1944 it hit a road bump. Wier explains in his book:

"...the farmers in Alpine were faced with a bountiful fruit harvest. However, the war had depleted the labor force and the farmers feared their harvest would end up rotting on the ground.

"The 200 fruit growers in the area...contacted the Michigan State University Extension Service to help them with their dilemma. The solution was establishing a camp of 400 prisoners of war near the village of Sparta."

In September, 1944, Army trucks delivered 400 German prisoners who had been captured from Rommel's Afrika Korps or in France after the Normandy Invasion. While Alpine men fought Hitler overseas, some of Hitler's soldiers were brought here to do the work of the Alpine men.

Each morning, the farmers would arrive at the concentration camp with trucks and haul from 10 to 15 prisoners to their orchards. The farmers would return the POWs in the evening.

Detroit Magazine, in a 1975 article, quoted grower Merlin Kraft, who was 18 at the time: "They were good workers. A hundred bushels of apples a day is considered a good day's picking. We had one prisoner here who consistently picked a hundred a day. When we asked him why he worked so hard, he said: 'So I can keep my mind off my wife and little girls.'"

National Czech & Slovak Museum & Library

Slovakia

CEDAR RAPIDS, Iowa – In December 1941, about the same time Japan attacked Pearl Harbor, the tiny Slovak Republic declared war on the United States and her allies.

Obviously, the United States had much bigger concerns -- such as entering World War II to face the major war powers of Japan and Germany. Slovakia wasn't even an issue. Why should it be? This Eastern European country was landlocked; it had no ships, and its military aircraft, if it had any, couldn't get across Europe yet alone the Atlantic Ocean to attack the United States.

Slovakia during World War II was in the hip pocket of Hitler's Nazi Germany. It had to do what Hitler told it to do. With German help, Slovak Republic declared its independence from Czechoslovakia on March 15, 1939. Germany didn't attack Slovakia as it did its close cousins the Czech Republic, but Hitler nevertheless pulled the strings of his puppet country. Hitler sent the Slovak Army to do his bidding attacking neighboring countries.

Ironically, Slovakia was headed at this time by a Roman Catholic priest, Father Josef Tisco, who delivered 70,000 Slovak Jews to the Nazis to be murdered in Auschwitz and other death camps. After the war, when Russia freed Slovakia from German rule, Tisco was tried for war crimes and hanged.

The rich histories of the Czechs and Slovaks are detailed through stories, pictures and drawings at the National Czech & Slovak Museum and Library here. How did Cedar Rapids land this national memorial featuring these two European countries?

The first Czech immigrant came to Cedar Rapids in the 1850s, and some 50 to 60 years later, one-third of Cedar Rapids' population were Czech immigrants and their families, said Jan Stoffer, the museum's director of programs and education. "It was a grassroots effort (to build the national museum); no one else (in the United States) did it," she said.

For many years, the Czech Fine Arts Foundation collected artifacts and books from Czechoslovakia. It first showcased them in a small house that the group converted into a museum.

Later, the town gave the museum board a long-term lease on property near the rambling Cedar River, and funds were raised to build this large museum. It was dedicated in 1995 by President Bill Clinton, Slovak President Michal Kovác and Czech President Václav Havel.

Stoffer said that although Cedar Rapids had a large Czech population, but hardly any Slovaks, the board decided to feature the history, culture and folk and fine arts of both countries.

The Czechs and Slovaks, both evolving from Slavic tribes centuries ago, were so closely related and were part of one country for many years that it just wouldn't seem right to leave the Slovaks out, Stoffer said.

She explained the Czechs migrated mostly to the heartland of America, including Texas, and many of them became farmers. The Slovaks, however, settled mostly in the eastern section of the United States near large cities. The majority of them worked in such industries as in steel mills and coal mines.

This is ironical because in Europe, the Czechs lived in an industrialized country and their neighbors, the Slovaks, lived in a farming country. The Slovaks, many of whom were peasants, mainly tilled their lands.

Bob Stone, a museum volunteer, explained that many Czechs in their homeland were involved in industry because there wasn't much private land to farm. But when they came to America, a lot of them played out their dreams and became farmers.

Another reason, said Stoffer, was the Czechs mainly came over to America with their families and could settle right away on farms. The Slovaks, rather, mainly came over alone and worked as steelworkers or miners and saved their money to bring their wives and children here later.

"The Slovaks were more migrant workers; (they) stayed in boarding houses," Stoffer said. "Czech families came united as family units; that meant Mom pressured Dad to buy a house and settle down."

Farm land in the late 1880s and early 1900s was relatively cheap in Iowa and surrounding states and this made it very attractive for immigrants.

Stoffer said that the Czech immigrants were more educated than the Slovaks. The Czechs came here with a 99 percent literacy rate. The Cedar Rapids Czechs started a school to teach the Czech language to their children. Before 1918, when Czechoslovakia was formed, German was taught in schools in the old country because the Czechs were under Austria rule.

"Mothers grounded their children in the Czech language, but at the same time committed and considered (themselves) wholehearted Americans," Stoffer said. However, the Slovak immigrants still held more of an allegiance to their homeland, she said.

One in every five Slovaks in the old country emigrated to the United States between 1880 and 1914, according to records displayed at the museum. "There are more Slovak-Americans, but more Czech-American communities in the United States," Stoffer said.

Visitors to the museum, in addition to learning the histories of the two peoples, will see such artifacts made out of dough, wheat straw and corn husks; wood carvings including a two-foot-long tobacco pipe; embroidered cloths; colorful folk costumes that include gold thread and intricate lace work; crystal sculptures; ceramic items; "splash-cloths" used over sinks; a classic motorcycle; World War I knife, bayonet and gas mask, and an antique printing press on which Czech language newspapers were printed for newly-arrived immigrants.

A two-room immigrant house originally build in 1885 in Cedar Rapids is located just outside the main building. It was moved to its present site in 1983 and restored and furnished to the 1880-90 period. At first, the house only had one room, about 160-square-feet, and the second room of equal size was added later. A family of five lived in it, with no plumbing. The only heat during harsh winters came from a wood/coal stove.

"Whether scholarly or merely curious, guests are welcome to explore the library's collection of books, periodicals, and archival materials in English, Czech, and Slovak," according to a museum brochure. "Library users will find a variety of materials on history, literature and art, as well as an extensive collection of recorded music and sheet music. The library's reading room allows visitors to browse through the English-language newspapers, *Prague Post* and *Slovak Spectator*, news from the Czech and Slovak embassies, publications from Czech and Slovak groups across the country, and many other materials of interest."

The gift shop features Czech and Slovak books, glassware, batik eggs, Modra ceramics, jewelry, costumed dolls, blown-glass ornaments, recorded music, language tapes, porcelain items, wooden toys and marionettes. You can also buy colorful button pins that implores: "Improve Your Image, Be Seen with a Slovak" or "Some People Are Married to Slovaks and Still Go On to Lead Normal Lives."

Nearby on a side street is Czech Village. There are stores selling ethnic artifacts, a couple bars, and Zindrick's Czech Restaurant. For Czech cuisine at its finest, try the cabbage rolls and Czech goulash.

Note: In June 2008, a massive flood devastated much of Cedar Rapids including the Czech and Slovak museum and library. Some of the collection was saved; others destroyed or damaged beyond repair. Plans to reconstruct are underway.

The Birthplace Visit

BETHLEHEM, Israel – It is hard to imagine that this town with soldiers standing around is where Jesus was born. Where's the inn and stable? Instead there is a large basilica, erasing the simplicity of the manger scene.

However, thousands of Christians around the world annually come to this hilltop Judean town a few miles south of Jerusalem to visit Jesus' birthplace.

The streets especially are jammed with Christian pilgrims Christmas Eve and Christmas Day. Many denominations conduct their own services in churches and shrines throughout the town.

They join together for a parade on Christmas Day.

But one Christian Arab guide who lives here likes to take visitors to a lookout point at the edge of this popular town.

He points to an excavation site of a former palace on top of a hill four miles away.

"That's King Herod's tomb," he says.

But who goes there to visit? Even in death, King Herod could not outshine his rival for the esteemed title of "King of the Jews."

The story of King Herod's hatred for Jesus is told in the second chapter of Matthew:

"Where is he that is born King of the Jews?" the three wise men asked King Herod. "For we have seen his star in the east, and are come to worship."

The biblical account says King Herod's chief priests and scribes told him the prophet Micah said the Christ will be born in Bethlehem. The king, who was jealous of anyone who was proclaimed "King of the Jews," sent the wise men to find Jesus and to return and tell him exactly where in the town the child lived.

The wise men found Jesus, worshiped Him, and gave Him gifts. They left, but did not see King Herod. An angel told Jesus' earthly father, Joseph, to flee to Egypt "for Herod will seek the young child to destroy Him."

King Herod was furious when he learned that the wise men had disobeyed him. He ordered soldiers to Bethlehem to kill every baby boy two years old and under. That way he was sure Jesus would be killed. But he was wrong. According to records, King Herod himself apparently died shortly after Jesus' birth...

The Arab guide points in another direction at the lookout point to the valley below.

"That's Shepherds' Field," he said. "The shepherds were there when Jesus was born."

The story of the shepherds is told in the second chapter of Luke:

"And there were in the same country shepherds abiding in the field, keeping watch over their flock by night."

An angel appeared before them and told them that "for unto you is born this day in the city of David a Savior, who is Christ the Lord..."

It is only a 5-minute walk from the lookout point to Manger Square in the heart of Bethlehem. Foremost is the Basilica of the Nativity, which is built over the place believed to be Jesus' birthplace. Israeli soldiers used to patrol this area for decades especially around Christmastime, but, since 2005, Bethlehem and other areas have been turned over to Palestinian authorities. With the change of guard, tourists are still permitted to visit here.

Since Jesus was born here 2,000 years ago, the town has changed hands many times. It had been ruled by Romans, Byzantines, Arabs, Crusaders, Mamelukes and Turks.

Despite the many centuries of frequently hostile non-Christian rule, which often made pilgrimages difficult and even hazardous, Christians have steadfastly clung to Bethlehem. It is among the most important of all Christian shrines.

The guide leads the way inside the basilica and down 13 well-worn cement steps to a grotto. He points to a marble slab with a 14-point gold star in the middle.

"Underneath there is the place where Jesus was born," he says.

Luke continues the story:

"And she (Mary) brought forth her first-born son, and wrapped him in swaddling clothes, and laid him in a manger, because there was no room for them in the inn.

The guide leads the way up the stairs and out to Manger Square where soldiers stand.

The story of the first Christmas – the birth of Jesus Christ – has endured in its simplicity for 2,000 years. Ironically, it wasn't Jesus' birth that made Christmas. It was his death. For without his death and resurrection, Christians wouldn't have hope. They never would have cherished Jesus' birth or birthplace.

And nearby King Herod's tomb, perhaps, would be more popular than Bethlehem today.

Jesus' Fishing Ministry

SEA OF GALILEE, Israel – More than 2,000 years ago, Jesus fished here --both for man and fish.

This 72-square-mile lake is shaped like a harp. Fishing methods have changed considerably since Jesus' time.

According to the Gospel of Luke, Jesus once told Simon where to cast a net on this sea to catch fish.

Simon, later named Peter, argued that he and other fishermen had toiled all night casting their nets and had not caught any fish. However, Simon obeyed Jesus, lowered his net into the sea and pulled in so many fish that his boat nearly sank.

Today, Israeli fishermen have their own high-tech method to catch fish in this barren body of water.

In the evening, they tow out unmanned boats, each carrying a powerful gas-mantle lamp to attract fish.

Hours later, a specially equipped boat with an electronic fish finder goes out to where the lightboats are anchored.

When the electronic finder locates a large concentration of fish, the boat's pilot radios the shore.

A seiner, or boat, comes from shore and lays a long nylon net around the lightboat that has lured the most fish. The fishermen use small power winches to haul in the net and fish.

Although the electronic age has changed the fishing here, the countryside around the lake since Jesus' time also has changed.

The shores of the sea are now dotted with ruins of old towns, indicating that during Jesus' days the area probably was more developed than it is today.

The Jewish historian Josephus, writing a few years after Christ's death, described the area as "a country of palaces smothered in balsam and scented bushes."

Today, as one looks at the lake and surrounding area from the top of a hill, the only town of any size is Tiberias on the west bank. The kibutz, Ein Gev, is on the east shore. A few buildings are scattered in between, but the vast terrain is barren – rolling hills and black boulders but with some patches of farmland.

The ancient towns – Capernaum, Bethsaida, Chorazin and others – have vanished.

Jesus condemned these three towns because they "repented not," although He displayed "mighty works" in the towns.

Jesus said: "And thou, Capernaum, which art exalted unto heaven, shalt be brought down to hell" (Matt. 11:23).

A sign outside the rubble of an ancient temple in Capernaum claims that this area was "the town of Jesus."

The Sea of Galilee is a magnet to Christian pilgrims.

Jesus often went into the surrounding hills to pray. He healed the sick in the villages.

It was here that He gave the Sermon on the Mount, fed the 5,000 with five loaves of bread and two fish, calmed the sea and walked on the water. He called some of the fishermen on this lake to join him and become his disciples. They did, dropping their nets and leaving their boats.

But most important to the Christian pilgrim, it was here that His message was preached; a message that has spread from these shores to around the world.

Journalists touring Sea of Galillee (circa 1970s). The author, right, in striped shirt.

Sea Of Cortez Rocks

LORETO, Mexico – A pleasant surprise awaited the 1,200 passengers after the Ryndam cruise ship sailed into harbor here. At other ports of calls, mainly on the Mexican Riveria and Cabo San Lucas, hawkers foisted gaudy trinkets on us after we got off ship. And, at Mazatlan, a fat American woman pressured passengers to take a free taxi ride to the American sector to attend a 90-minute time-share, arm-twisting presentation.

At Loreto, however, the townspeople gathered in the plaza for a fiesta – a special show just for the passengers. Children from the local school performed folk dances, a small band played, and women in elaborate costumes danced. Other women sang solos. And, all this was free.

Loreto residents don't see that many cruise-line tourists. Only Holland America's Ryndam ship comes here about three times a month from October through April. This is part of a 10-day cruise that starts (and ends) at San Diego and includes six ports of call – Puerto Vallarta, Mazatlan and Cabo San Lucas that is considered part of the Mexican Riveria, and Los Mochis (via Topolobampo), La Paz (via Pichilingue) and Loreto in the Sea of Cortez.

The three Sea of Cortez ports are the high point of the

Loreto's main street

cruise. They just aren't as touristy and spoiled, yet!

Loreto, with a population of about 10,000, has a rich history. Spanish explorers first arrived here in 1533. Pericu Indians inhabited the area. They survived by collecting fruit, hunting and fishing. The Jesuit missionaries established the Baja peninsula's first mission (in a makeshift tent) here in 1697, making Loreto the historic capital of California and Baja California until 1777.

The Nuestro Senora de Loreto church (Our Lady of Loreto) was built in 1752 and has since been repaired many times due to hurricanes, earthquakes and floods. It stands today in the center of town. Displayed inside is Padre Juan Maria Salvaatierra's original Virgen de Loreto, brought ashore in 1697. Adjacent to the church is Museo de las Misiones, displaying historic and religious artifacts mostly relating to Baja California peninsula.

The main attractions at the ports of call towns are the beaches, clear and warm waters, snorkeling, scuba-diving, kayak rowing, whale-watching (January through March),

Costumed dancer in Loreto

golfing and year-round fishing. Shops abound featuring jewelry, colorful clothing and tons of souvenirs from pottery and wooden statues of animals to blankets and purses. Then there are restaurants galore with fish and shrimp being king.

Once on shore, the cruise passenger has a plethora of excursions to take. Many prefer to hoof it and explore the marketplaces, cathedrals, museums, shops, parks and beaches on their own. Or, you can book an excursion at the ship's front desk, or from Holland America in advance. Here are some selections from these six ports-of-call:

Loreto – A guided walking tour; horseback ride following a stream bed, Mexican fiesta (live music and ballet folklorico dancers) and clambake and a trip to the rustic San Javier mission 23 miles from town.

Los Mochis – The ship anchors at Topolobampo, the third naturally deep port in the world behind Sidney, Australia, and San Francisco. The highlight for the first 400 people to sign up is the train ride to the vast Copper Canyon (Mexico's version of the Grand Canyon) that traverses over numerous bridges and through many tunnels. While at canyon's edge, walk down to the caves where Tarahumara Indians live. They sell handmade souvenirs, and also perform folk dances. Plan for a full day, and much of the night, for the trip -- six hours on the train each way, plus a few more hours on a bus. Passengers leave the ship at 4:30 a.m., arriving back at about 10 p.m.

For those left behind, a short bus ride takes passengers to Los Mochis, where a guided tour visits a sugar cane factory (just the outside of it), a botanical garden with trees from around the world (Royal palm has concrete-looking bark and banyan tree from India with roots growing straight-down from its limbs), museums, cathedral and marketplace. Or, you can take a river float trip, visit a small Indian village and a mango plantation hacienda, or take a boat cruise to spot dolphins.

La Paz – In addition to a self-guided tour of the town, cruise tourists can visit El Serpentario Reptile Center (featuring albino cobras, giant pythons and lizards, turtles/tortoises and crocodiles), go kayaking, travel 1½ miles to Todos Santos, a picturesque town overlooking the Pacific Ocean and blessed with green crops, palm groves and mango and avocado trees. Also, see a pottery factory, learn about the colors and characteristics of Sea of Cortez pearls (found only in La Paz), snorkel or scuba dive.

Puerto Vallarta – Highly recommended is the bus tour of the city that includes how tequila is made and see from a bus Elizabeth Taylor's former house. You also can see the countryside on horseback, swim with the dolphins, glide through the treetops on a network of cables suspended above the tropical forest, Sierra Madre hiking adventure (take a dip in a volcanic hot water spring), and pirate ship snorkel and sail adventure (you can also do this at Cabo San Lucas).

Mazatlan – Walk the streets of old town and especially visit the huge marketplace featuring butcher shops with meat on top of the counter, and an array of every souvenir imaginable.

Raw meat sold in Mazatlan marketplace

You can also visit the Pacifico Brewery (arguably the best of all Mexican beer), attend a shrimp fest, tour the rustic village of Malpica where floor tiles are made, see the Papantla Flyers, daredevil Totonac Indians who ascend a 75-foot pole and descend on ropes spinning around the pole back to the ground, take a boat to bird watch, and participate in "Salsa & Salsa," which includes making your own margarita and salsa and then learn the salsa dance.

Cabo San Lucas – Be prepared when you get off ship and walk to downtown to be accosted by a bevy of hawkers (they even blow whistles so they would draw more attention to themselves.). There are many restaurants along shore but walk into town. At Poncho's you can relax and enjoy

Hole-in-rock at Cabo San Lucas

Mexican cuisine. You even may be entertained by two roving guitar-playing singers. One may wear a false mustache. Give a healthy tip and they will sing another song for free. Also at Cabo, you can ride horseback on the beach, kayak and snorkel, go ATVing, take a jeep ride to La Candelaria, a small oasis village in the middle of the desert, whale-watching (January-March), and, if you are an angler, get on one of the 100 sportfishing boats and practice catch-and-release fishing.

The Ryndam leaves Cabo at 4 p.m. and it is formal night in the dining room. On a personal note, I ate the best filet mignon and lobster I've ever had in my life. The dining staff puts on an elaborate celebration serving guests baked Alaskan dessert. Picture sparklers spraying sparks all over the place.

What a way to end a sparkling Mexican vacation!

Secluded Paradise

TYINHOLMEN, Norway – When I arrived in Oslo completely drained, tired of train rides to big cities, brushing shoulders with strangers on the streets and desperately needing to get away from another big city, I sought respite.

"Where can I go to get away from crowds of pushing people, jungles of concrete buildings, honking cars and somewhere that is cheap?" I asked a Norwegian woman at the Oslo's American Embassy.

"Try Tyinholmen in Jotunheimen."

"I beg your pardon!"

"Tyinholmen is a secluded place on a lake in the Jotunheimen mountains. You'd love it there," she assured me.

A few hours later I boarded a train for Fagernes, 120 miles northwest of Oslo and the last town of any size before entering Jotunheimen, a 2,700 square-mile hikers' playground in the center of Norway. It's covered with 250 peaks 6,000 feet and above, 60 glaciers and countless rivers, lakes, valleys, narrow passes and mountain farms.

Settling in a tilt-back seat next to a huge window, the cement jungle quickly disappeared into forests of pines and birch and green meadows with purple wildflowers. Cows stood knee-deep munching grass.

A small blue lake appeared. Then another and another. Green islands, some so tiny only three or four saplings could grow on them, barely poked out of the water. Tiny villages in fertile valleys sped by.

Fagernes is the end of the line. Tyinholmen is another 70 miles away. The lofty and mysterious Jotunheimen beckoned, and a bus waited to take me there. The paved road from town quickly turned into a dusty, but well-maintained dirt road. This is when one realizes that the rugged beauty of Norway is king here – and memories of concrete buildings, crowds of people and honking cars start to fade.

The bus driver doubles as mailman and makes frequent stops at villages to deliver and pick up mail. The bus trip, that snakes through valleys alongside lakes, rivers and small villages lasts 2 ½ hours, including a rest stop at Grindaheim ("herrer" is men, "damer" women).

It isn't until the last half-hour that the bus climbs and it is here that the majestic snow-capped Jotunheimen peaks can first be seen. Tyinholmen, on a seven-mile-long Lake Tlyin, lies at their base.

Tyinholmen is one of the largest mountain resort areas in the Jotunheimen, its main lodge can accommodate 125 people. Since it is off the beaten tourist path, it is hardly necessary to write ahead for reservations. Cost for a room is cheaper than in hotels in large cities.

Breakfast and lunch are smorgasbord style – all you can eat. A typical breakfast consists of eggs, bacon, hash brown potatoes, oatmeal, dry cereals, fruit juice, grapefruit, coffee or tea, variety of lunch meats, potato cakes, various cheeses, six kinds of fish, prunes, beets, applesauce, salads, a variety of rolls, bread and crackers and various flavors of jelly and jam.

The only difference with lunch is that there is a wider selection of foods including as many fresh and delicious strawberries in a thick cream a person can eat.

Mostly hiking enthusiasts from throughout Scandinavia, Holland and England come to Tyinholmen. According to the resort's manager, very few Americans come here, by-passing Jotunheimen for the more famous fjord area in the south.

Most guests leave early each morning for day-long excursions to conquer one of the peaks or explore a glacier. The Norwegian Mountain Touring Association has cairned and placed signposts along the network of paths throughout Jotunheimen.

Some people, though, just rest on the patio and get a tan while looking at a glacier sandwiched by two snow-covered peaks less than a mile away. A few of the hearty take a dip in the ice-cold lake.

Surprisingly, most summer days are short-sleeved weather, although nights require a sweater or jacket.

The lodge provides row boats for its guests. A leisurely morning or afternoon can be spent drifting on the quiet and almost ripple-free lake.

After dinner, served by half-dozen attractive Norwegian girls working and living at the lodge during the summer season, guests usually spend the waning hours in the lounge and bar dancing to live folk music and swapping tales of the day's hiking experiences. For most of the guests, English is their second language.

Or, if you feel like a limp rag, the lodge has a Finnish sauna to put new life into your tired limbs.

Throughout Jotunheimen are a number of small chalets and hotels. Serious hikers spend days walking from one lodge to another exploring the peaks, glaciers, lakes, streams and valley farms along the way. The Jostedalsbreen, on the western end, is the largest glacier in Europe.

I spent four days at Tyinholmen and on the day I left, the manager drove me two miles to Eidsbugaren to climb into a boat. He suggested a new scenic boat-bus route to Fagernes through parts of Jotunheimen.

At Eidsbugaren, the 75-foot Bitihorn boat knives 15 miles -- the length of the finger-like Lake Bygdin. The trip takes 1 ½ hours, but the scene is constantly changing as the Mighty Jotunheimen peaks slowly pass in review.

Half-way, the boat stops at a tiny lakeside chalet. A young couple wearing knapsacks step off and carefully start their way up a lonely trail to the mysterious heart of Jotunheimen.

The inky waters at this point are almost 700 feet deep, the captain says. As the boat nears the far end of the lake, the Jotunheimen fades from view. A bus waits on shore to take passengers 33 miles to Fagernes.

Later that day, I got off the train at Oslo – refreshed, a little heavier, and eager to explore another European capital.

Jotunheimen works wonders on one's psyche.

Outbuildings at Jotunheimen lake. (circa 1960s)

Another Fish Story

This book's title relates to my earlier fish story in Part 1 – Snippets of Life. I hope you enjoyed that yarn, which is purely a creation of my imagination. Thus, in keeping with the book's title, I thought I would write another fish story that, instead, is absolutely 100 percent true. The picture on the next page is a large building shaped like a fish and people can walk inside. Thus, like Jonah, people are inside a "fish" –a fish really catches man, so to speak!

Hayward, Wisconsin -- Northwest Wisconsin is a fisherman's haven. In Hayward, where the National Fresh Water Fishing Hall of Fame is located, you can stand in the open mouth of a muskellunge (Musky) fish and overlook nearby Hayward Lake and the City of Hayward.

This Musky is man-built, 4 ½-stories high and spans a half of a city block. You can walk inside the "fish" and view various fish exhibits including mounted fish, along the climb to the fish's mouth.

Beneath the Musky is a reflection pool that is stocked annually with various species of fish and turtles from area lakes and rivers. This usually includes northern pike, bass, bluegill, sunfish, white sucker, redhorse sucker and painted turtles.

Fish building in Hayward

This hall of fame sits on seven acres and includes other display buildings, landscaped grounds, a gift shop, snack lounge and statues of various species of fish.

There are also 400 fish mounts that features 200 species of fish, 5,000 fishing lures, more than 600 classic and antique outboard motors and hundreds of vintage fishing reels and fishing accessories. Also, you can try your luck to reel in a lunker at the fishing pond.

Some of the displays include Seminole Indian fishing arrows, an antique ice fishing display, a rare 1929 Wisconsin Game Warden's uniform and a copy of the first English writing on the subject of fishing entitled *Here Begynnth The Treatise of Fishynge With an Angle,* originally written in 1496.

The blue game warden uniform was styled after the Royal Canadian Mounted Police's red uniform. It was even made from the same fabric as the Mounties. The state changed the color to forest green the next year and the short-lived "blue Mountie" uniform was moth-balled.

If it wasn't for Jim Beam whiskey distillers of Chicago and

Kentucky, there may have never been the fish hall of fame. The idea for the museum began in the 1960s and a goal of $1 million was needed to get it started. Funding by government agencies and the fishing industry didn't materialize. That's when the Jim Beam people offered a multi-year program to raise funds from the national sale of collector fish decanters. The first Beam decanter was issued in 1971, and netted $28,000 for the museum. When the Beam program ended in the 1980s, net proceeds to the museum resulted with about $250,000. By this time other donations from mostly local businesses and individuals and from gate receipts kept the museum afloat and allowed it to expand.

The museum is open seven days a week from April 15 to Nov. 1.

While in northern Wisconsin, check out other things to see and do. Hunting is a tremendous sport up here. Game consists of grouse, crow, partridge, dove and Canada goose to black bear, white-tailed deer, beaver, fox and coyote. There are certain seasons for these animals. However, the opossum, skunk, weasel and snowshoe hare should watch out. There are no season limits, bag limits, size limits or possession limits on these creatures.

Tourists can take scenic canoe and tube trips, visit numerous historical museums, attend lumberjack shows, take a ferry to Madeline Island, sip Muskie Merlot at Hook Stone Winery in Hayward, visit Al Capone's hideout, party at apple and cranberry festivals in early October, hike interpretive trails and drive the Fall color tours in the pine and hardwood forests of the area.

And above all, for Pete's sake, buy some Wisconsin cheese to take home. The varieties are endless from Swiss, brick, cheddar, Gouda to feta, Havarti, Monterey jack and limburger. There is a new line called Braun Suisse Kase, made of 100 percent certified Brown Swiss cow's milk. One cheese shop even stocks "chocolate fudge" cheese.

States of Confusion

Living in the United States is mighty confusing.

Let's take my adopted home state of Arizona. Please! If you lived in the town of Maricopa, you wouldn't live in Maricopa County, but in Pinal County. And, if your residence is the community of Navajo, you live in Apache County. And, if you settled in Fort Apache, you'd be in Navajo County.

And, as might be expected, Apache Junction isn't in Apache County, but in Pinal County. And, continuing the confusion, Gila Bend missed being in Gila County by 135 miles. It's in Maricopa County.

Geronimo was one of the country's most celebrated Apache warriors. There's a town named after him. It misses being on an Indian reservation by two miles. The town of Pima fits well into Arizona's strange geographical pattern. It is in Graham County, not Pima County.

There are two towns named Carrizo in Arizona. One is in the Navajo reservation and the other is in an Apache Indian sector. The towns of San Jose, Alamo and Klondike are in Arizona. And, where else in the world can you find more unusual names of creeks, mountains, washes, and various landmarks such as Devils Wind Pipe Canyon, Elephants Tooth, Freezeout Creek, Bloody Tanks, Cowlic, Big Bug,

Battleship Mountain, Fourth of July Wash, Grief Hill, Gunsight Well, Lousy Gulch, Monkey Springs, Methodist Creek, Spud Rock and Camelback.

And then there are such communities as Mud Springs, Gu Achi, Gu Oidak and Gu Vo.

Enough said of Arizona. I was so fascinated with this state of confusion that I decided to look at other states as well. They are just as messed up as Arizona. *(Author's note: Granted, when I did this grueling, and some may say useless, research many years ago, I not only had too much time on my hands but at the time I had no life at all.)*

Illinois – The town of Hardin is the county seat of Calhoun County, not Hardin County. And, Marshall isn't the county seat of Marshall County, but Clark County. As might be expected, Clinton and Marion are not the heads of government for Clinton and Marion Counties. They're of DeWitt and Williamson counties.

And do you think Edwardsville, Carrollton and McLeansboro are in Edwards, Carroll and McLean counties respectively. Nope! They all are in other counties. And Whiteash, White City, Whitefield, White Hall, White Heath and White Pines are not in White County.

Only in the Land of Lincoln, and not going out-of-state, could Chicago be closer to Paris, Palestine and Rome than to Nashville. And, in Illinois, Brooklyn is less than 15 miles from Tennessee. The man in charge of naming creeks in Pike County made a mistake while pacing off Sixmile Creek. On the state map it weaves closer to 20 miles.

If you don't want to leave the state, you can still visit Wyoming, Oregon, Ohio, Kansas, Virginia, Phoenix, Pittsburg, Atlanta, Peru, Panama, Belgium, Bunker Hill, Havana and Cuba. You guessed it! They're all Illinois communities.

Scattered throughout the state are at least five Sugar creeks, four Otter creeks, four Rock creeks, three Hickory creeks, three Camp creeks, two Horseshoe lakes and two Kickapoo creeks.

Michigan – Detroit is closer to Athens than to Wyoming.

And, Nashville and Portland are only about 25 miles apart. The settlement of Southbranch is north of North Branch. The town of St Joseph is the county seat of Berrien County, not St. Joseph County. And, Mason is the county seat of Ingham County, not Mason County.

If you don't want to leave the state you can still visit Atlanta, Augusta, Norway, St. Louis, Brooklyn, Birmingham, Memphis, Rochester and Moscow. You guessed it! They're all Michigan communities.

Michigan has at least five Pine rivers and four Black rivers. And landmarks include Cat Head, Zug, Tittabawassee, Tahquamernon, Potoganissing, Ontonagon, Munuscong, Raisin, Rifle, Shot and Conglomerate. Then there are such communities at Bath, Climax, De Tour, Fruitport, Maybee, Paw Paw, Pigeon, White Pigeon, Saugatuck, Romeo, Three Oaks, Three Rivers, White Cloud, Frankenmuth, Dowagiac, Onekama, Newaygo, Sebewaing, Temperance and Zilwaukee (not to be confused with Milwaukee).

Iowa – This state has a mix-up in county-seat names, too. The towns of Jefferson, Osceola, Wapello, Des Moines and Sioux City are not heads of government of Jefferson, Osceola, Wapello, Des Moines and Sioux counties, but, respectively, of Greene, Clarke, Louisa, Polk and Woodbury counties.

To add to the confusion, the towns of Fremont, Greene, Keokuk, Marion, Monona and Monroe aren't in their namesake counties either.

Only in the Hawkeye State can Des Moines be closer to Madrid than to Knoxville. And Madrid and Knoxville are less than 60 miles apart. And, Buffalo and Wyoming are about 50 miles apart. The towns of Cincinnati, Birmingham, Brooklyn, Nevada, Toledo, Akron, Dayton, Denver and Oakland are all in Iowa.

On a state map, Sevenmile Creek is 30 miles long. There are two Little Turkey rivers, three Swan lakes and two Goose lakes in Iowa. Unusual town names in the state: Morning Sun, What Cheer, Mystic, Lone Tree, Coon Rapids, Correctionville, Kanawha, Pocahontas, Oskaloosa and Keosauqua.

Ohio -- Okay, let's get it out of the way quickly. Neither the towns of Sandusky or Upper Sandusky are the county seat of Sandusky County. They're of Erie and Wyandot counties respectively. And, Jefferson, Hamilton, Logan, Ottawa and Warren are not heads of government for Jefferson, Hamilton, Logan, Ottawa and Warren counties. They're of Ashtabula, Butler, Hocking, Putnam and Trumbull counties.

If you live in the town of Valley View, you would be living in either Cuyahoga or Franklin counties. There are two Valley Views in Ohio. Also, to the dismay of post office officials, there also are two towns of Belmont, Oakwood and Shiloh.

Only in the Buckeye state can Cleveland be closer to Poland and Vienna than to Buffalo and Grand Rapids. And, would you believe that Holland is less than 20 miles from Oregon? All those places are in Ohio. If you don't want to leave the state, you can still visit Baltimore, Brooklyn, Cairo, Damascus, Delaware, Lisbon, London, Louisville, Nevada, Toronto, Athens, Antwerp and Wyoming (it seems Wyoming is in just about every state in the union).

Kentucky – North Middletown is south of Middletown, and West Liberty is 100 miles northeast of Liberty. Boston and Texas, two Bluegrass State towns, are only about 45 miles apart.

If you don't want to leave the state, you can still visit London, Mexico, Bagdad, Paris and Washington. You guessed it, again! They're all Kentucky communities. Kentucky men sure must love their womanfolk. Where else are towns named Betsy Layne, Cecilia, Florence, Cynthiana, Hazel, Hazel Green, Lola Louisa, Mary, Nancy, Rosine and Ruth.

On a state map, Sixmile Creek weaves closer to 20 miles before emptying into the Kentucky River. Short Creek in Grayson County is longer than Long Creek in Lyon and Trigg counties.

Where in the world can you find more unusual names of towns, creeks, forks, rivers, mountains, reservoirs, dams and runs. Only in Kentucky (and other states as you've been reading)! Here are a few: Stinking, Corn, Peter, Troublesome,

Kinniconick, Cub Run, New Hope, Hi Hat, Flat Lick, Crab Orchard, Pippa Passes, Oldtown, Stamping Ground and Summer Shade.

And, did you think you would get out of Kentucky without seeing the customary screw-ups in county names. Nope! The towns of Hickman, Clinton, Grayson, Marion, Carlisle and Franklin are all county seats. But not any of them are in Hickman, Clinton, Grayson, Marion, Carlisle and Franklin counties.

California – Ho-hum! Let's go again. Yuba City is the county seat of Sutter County and Placerville is the county seat of El Dorado County. There are Yuba and Placer counties in this state.

Whew! I'm glad we got that over with. Wait! Alpine and San Joaquin are not in Alpine and San Joaquin counties. They're in San Diego and Fresno counties respectively.

The town of Lucerne is more than 425 miles northwest of the town of Lucerne Valley. And, the town of Portola (north of Lake Tahoe) is about 240 miles northeast of Portola Valley, just south of San Francisco.

Women are also honored in the Golden Bear state. Landmarks include Eleanor Lake, Georgiana Slough (Okay, maybe some guy hated Georgiana), Gertrude Lake, Emma Mountain, Florence Lake, Dixie Mountain, Isabella Dam, Jenny Creek, Josephine Mountain, Mary Lake, Shirley Mountain, Susan River, Virginia Creek and Wanda Lake.

There are at least five Black mountains in the state along with five Dry creeks, four Willow creeks, four Mill creeks and two Twin lakes and Twin peaks. There is a Mount Ararat in California (El Dorado County). It can be safely said it is not the same Mount Ararat mentioned in Genesis where Noah's ark finally came to rest. That one is in Turkey.

How would you like to live in Shingle Springs? How about Feather Falls, Fellows, Fawnskin and Angels Camp? They are all California towns.

Minnesota – Tenmile Lake in Cass County is more that twice the size of Ten Mile Lake in Otter Tail County. Otter

Tail! Would you want to tell your out-of-state friends that you live in Otter Tail? Yuk! Or, you can tell your friends you are a Fertile resident. Fertile, along with Coon Rapids, Harmony, Plato, Good Thunder and Sleepy Eye are Minnesota towns.

Scattered throughout the vast state are at least 21 Long lakes, 15 Rice lakes, eight Round lakes, six Eagle lakes and six Cedar lakes. Animals are popular in the Gopher State. There are Bald Eagle Lake, Bear Creek, Bear Island, Bear Lake, Bear River, Big Bat Lake, Elephant Lake, Deer Lake, Crow Lake, Cat River, Horse Lake, Fox Lake, Turtle Lake, Rabbit Lake, Pelican Lake and Toad Lake.

Women have equal status with animals. Consider: Isabella River, Elizabeth Lake, Ann River, Lucille Island, Emily Lake, Belle Creek, Sarah Lake, Rose Creek, Sandy River, Lillian Lake, Sylvia Lake, Lizzie Lake and Nina Moose Lake. And not to offend any of the state's females not named here, one lake was simply named Women Lake.

The stately red pine may be Minnesota's state tree, but the common maple gets a lot of attention. Six towns are named after it: Maple Grove, Maple Lake, Maple Plain, Mapleton, Mapleview and Maplewood.

I could tell you that the town of Marshall is the county seat of Marshall County. But I won't. It's the county seat of Lyon County. And, the same with Faribault, the head of government of Rice County. Yes, there is a Faribault County in the state.

Georgia -- What's with names of Georgia's county-seats that differ from towns of the same names elsewhere in the state? There are 20 towns that are the heads of governments of counties not their namesakes. Monroe is the county seat of Walton County, not Monroe County. Etc., 19 more times.

While on the same subject, there is an Oglethrope County in Georgia, but the town of Oglethorpe is in Macon County, Mt. Oglethorpe is in Dawson County and Oglethorpe University is in DeKalb County.

If you don't want to leave the state you can still visit Berlin, Cairo, Dallas, Duluth, Louisville, Rome and Vienna.

They are all in the Peach State. Boston, a Georgia town, is only about 50 miles away from Nashville, another Georgia town.

I could tell you that Tenmile Creek runs about 20 miles, that there are at least six Cedar creeks and there are towns named Lizella, Climax, Dacula, Doctortown and Sand Fly. But, I...guess I just did. Yep! They are all in Georgia.

Missouri – There are a bunch of towns in the state that are county seats, but not of their namesake counties. Period!

Only in the Show-me State Hollywood and Holland are less than 20 miles apart. If you don't leave the state you can still visit Atlanta, California, Cuba, Denver, Houston, Louisiana, Mexico, Miami, Nevada, Oregon and Washington. Missouri can't make up its mind. There are three Clear creeks and three Muddy creeks in the state.

How would you like to live in Neck City, Fair Play, Blue Eye, Blue Lick, Bourbon, Climax Springs, Bellefontaine Neighbors, Sleeper, Moscow Mills or Town & Country? They are all in Missouri.

Missouri is a green state. Communities include Green Acres, Green Castle, Green City, Green Ridge, Greendale, Greenfield, Greentop, Greenville and Greenwood.

New York – The towns of Cattaraugus, Chautauqua and Wyoming (not again!) are in Cattaraugus, Chautauqua and Wyoming counties respectively. But none of them are county seats.

Only in the Empire State can New York City be closer to Florida and Cleveland than to Boston and Philadelphia. And would you believe that Holland and Wyoming are about 25 miles apart; Madrid and Bombay about 30 miles apart, and Rome and Phoenix about 40 miles apart. All of these places mentioned in this paragraph are in New York.

If you don't want to leave the state, you can still visit Poland, Mexico, Cairo, Copenhagen, Cuba, Maine, Maryland, Naples, Panama, Peru, Youngstown, Athens, Amsterdam and Berlin.

There's a town of East Aurora, but it is west of the town of

Aurora. East Hampton is about 265 miles southeast of Hampton, and East Norwich is 165 miles southeast of Norwich.

For those New Yorkers who like to drop a name or two, string 18 New York communities together and come up with: Randolph Scottsville, Sherman Adams, Alexander Hamilton, De Witt Clinton, Lyndonville Johnson City, Georgetown Washingtonville, Williamson Harrison and Theresa Brewerton.

Also in the state is a Fivemile creek and a Five Mile Creek. Do you want to live in Fishkill, Great Neck, Deposit, Endwell, Bath or Bliss? You can in New York.

(Author's note: I hope I never will have too much time on my hands again. There are still 39 more state maps I could tackle)

Part Four – About This Book

The Meeting

I scooted into a booth at a Phoenix café, ordered two coffees, one for me and one for Erin.

Erin is a college student in Arizona State University's Walter Cronkite School of Journalism. I had sent my manuscript to ASU last month and hoped someone would write something nice to promote *Fish Catches Man*.

Erin called couple days ago and said she was assigned to write a book review, and she chose to read my book. She had some questions, though.

The door opened, and a cute young woman entered the café. I immediately felt old meeting someone young enough to be my granddaughter.

Since I was the only customer in the café, Erin walked to my booth, scooted in opposite me and slid the manuscript across the table.

"I read your manuscript, and I'm totally confused what you were trying to do with it," she began. "Is it fiction or non-fiction?"

"Yes," I said.

"What?"

"It's both," I explained. "You go into a Borders or Barnes & Noble and you will see thousands of books. Everyone and his or her grandmother are writing books nowadays. I wanted to write something that is outside the box."

"So, it's a collection of short stories both fact and fiction?" she asked. "Don't you know no one is reading short stories these days?"

"You're right," I said. "The short-story market has dried up. People want to read novels, not short stories. They think they are getting more for their money with long, involved plots and detailed characterizations and descriptions."

"So you have one or two strikes against you from the git-go."

"I know. I have been writing for more than 50 years and I wrote one story in the book while attending ASU, when I was about your age. None of the articles are heavy reading, but a glimpse at a certain time in a person's life. A snippet of life, sort-of-speak."

"Well, you covered all bases, I suppose," Erin said. "The stories were fast-moving and yet some were disturbing and some made me smile and even laugh out loud."

"That's exactly what I tried to do. I wanted the reader to have some reaction when they finished a story. The People and Places sections are 100 percent true, or non-fiction. Well, I did make some stuff up about my editor in the George Burns story. Part One – Snippets of Life, is a combination of fact and fiction. Some stories are made-up things out of my imagination. Other stories are partly true and partly fiction, only names, places, quotes and what's happening changed or embellished. So, if it isn't 100 percent fact than it has to be classified as fiction."

"Well," Erin said, "a few of the stories really stirred me. I felt I was part of what was going on. I really felt for the main characters."

She paused for a moment, and then said:

"There is one thing, though, you lacked in your book."

"What's that?"

"Most books have a lot of stuff such as an introduction, dedication, forward, acknowledgements, bibliography, preface and so on. You don't."

"I wanted the reader get to the heart of the book immediately and not wade through an introduction and acknowledgements and preface and all that boring stuff. I don't know why publishers put that stuff in front of the book. I'm having all of that in the end of my book. It wasn't in the manuscript I sent you. Advance copies of the book came out yesterday. I have a signed copy for you and I'll give you one when this interview is finished."

"Okay, for my review for the school paper, please clue me in."

"I think I already explained the introduction part. The book is dedicated to my immediate family, my wife Dawn, daughter Rachel, son Derek and his wife Amanda, and my two precious granddaughters, Nicole and Kyrie. Also, I want to acknowledge my former employers, *The Arizona Republic, Milwaukee Journal* and International Minerals & Chemical Corporation. Some information about people and places I wrote for these publications dating back to the 1960s I used in my book. I edited information from the original source for this book. I acknowledge these companies for the opportunity to meet and write about many interesting people, and visit some great places in the United States and other countries.

"I also want to thank my friend Bob David, a fish biologist who ran two fish hatcheries on the Fort Apache Indian Reservation, who helped me get inside the head of a fish. My wife, Dawn, and I took most of the pictures in the book. A few other pictures I used were sent out years earlier for press purposes. My daughter, a self-employed interior designer, created the front cover, and both she and my wife edited the book."

Erin reached for the manuscript on the table and began thumbing through it.

"I noticed a lot of the stories are religious," she said. "Are you religious?"

"Some people may think so, but I don't like the label of being called religious," I said. "There was a time in my life in my 20s and early 30s I had very little to do with God and the church. I probably was an agnostic. I lived a selfish life seeking worldly pleasures that were contrary to God's Holy Book. That world crashed for me in January 1970 when I realized I was going down a hazardous and self-destructive path. A friend gave me some spiritual literature and after spending several hours reading it, and listening to a Christian tape recording, I knew what I had to do.

"I prayed and accepted Jesus Christ as my Lord and Savior. I'm not religious, but I do have a personal relationship with the Lord. Everything hinges on this relationship. I'm not saying I'm some sort of a saint, because I still mess up. I know the love and forgiveness I have since I turned my life over to Jesus Christ. I know what my life was before Christ, and what my life is now. You can't compare the two."

Erin sat there not saying a word. She closed the manuscript and put it in her large purse.

"I think I now understand where you are coming from," she finally said. "What you have written now makes more sense to me."

"Let me ask you a question," I said. "What is the story that struck you the most?"

Without hesitation, she answered:

"*Little Buddy*. And I guess *Fish Catches Man* in second place. That fish story is really weird, though."

"Why did you like *Little Buddy*?" I asked.

"I was in a relationship that turned sour and I got a puppy to help me get through it. I related to that *Little Buddy* story, but I was sad at your ending."

"Well, like I said earlier, I want each of my stories to leave the readers with some kind of an impact, an emotional response."

"I think you accomplished that," Erin said. "I also liked the O'Henry ending of the boy who ran away from home."

"That story was totally based on a painting by Norman Rockwell," I said. "It's called *The Runaway* and I just made up a story from that scene. I contacted the Rockwell family and asked for permission to use that illustration to go with my story, but they e-mailed back saying it was against their policy to allow Norman Rockwell's paintings to appear in self-published books. But you can Google and see the painting. It's all over the internet."

"I'll do it," Erin said. "That reminds me of another thing; you used real photographs of real people to illustrate a fictitious story."

"As I said, I wanted this book to be out of the box. These pictures are solely for illustrated purposes only and any relation between the people in the pictures and those in the stories are strictly coincidental."

We said our good-bys, and I handed her a copy of the first printing of *Fish Catches Man*.

Three hours later, I got a frantic telephone call from Erin.

"Our interview today is in your book. How did that happen? You had my copy with you all the time. I'm confused."

I smiled.

"Well, Erin. It's one of the mysteries of self-publishing, especially when the author has complete control of everything in his book. Fact and fiction are interwoven in some of the stories. Did our interview ever taken place?"

"Yes," she said, still a bit confused. "I forgot to thank you for the coffee. I remember I didn't like it, and you really are handsome for your age."

"Thanks," I said. "I doubt any editor or publisher would let me get away with all of this. Like I said, this book "is outside the box."

TOP O' THE PINES
Life in Pinetop
and the White Mountains

by
Gene Luptak

Ponderosa Pine Press
Pinetop, Arizona

John Phipps in 1885 traveled on a rutted wagon trail from the Fort Apache Indian Reservation. He found a meadow with bubbling springs and cascading creeks. There, he set down stakes and built a saloon. Thus, Pinetop had its first resident. Arizona's White Mountains are filled with history and mystery – a pristine land tamed by sheepmen, cattlemen, Mormon pioneers, lumbermen, freighters and farmers. It also had its share of renegade outlaws. Apaches and their ancestors roamed this area for centuries.

Gene Luptak wrote a history of Pinetop and the White Mountains, a top tourist spot in the state. Hiking trails, lakes, streams, hunting, fishing and skiing abound among the towering Ponderosa trees.

Make a place on your shelf for *Top O' The Pines*, and you can read it over and over again. The book makes great gifts for family and friends -- anyone who has even a remote interest in the White Mountains. For a copy of *Top O' The Pines* or *Fish Catches Man*, send $17 each (which includes postage, shipping and handling) to: Gene Luptak, P.O. Box 296, Pinetop, AZ 85935

Top O' The Pines, 190 pages ISBN 0-9759005-0-1
Fish Catches Man, 280 pages ISBN 978-0-9759005-1-2
Ponderosa Pine Press, Pinetop, Az
booksmart@hotmail.com

www.ingramcontent.com/pod-product-compliance
Lightning Source LLC
Chambersburg PA
CBHW071123170626
46809CB00002B/477